Children of Nowhere

L. Steele

Published by L. Steele, 2024.

This is a work of fiction. Similarities to real people, places, or events are entirely coincidental.

CHILDREN OF NOWHERE

First edition. December 22, 2024.

Copyright © 2024 L. Steele.

ISBN: 979-8227579720

Written by L. Steele.

Chapter One –

1

"Choroes...Choroes...Choroes?"

Jessa had never even heard of this brand of potato chips before, much less knew what they looked like. However she had no choice but to keep searching because if she went back with the wrong ones, Elle would pitch a fit. Substitutions just weren't accepted when it came to Elle – something they had all learnt within a few days of moving into the share house and discovered her 'ground rules' and chore-chart implementation. Elle had had also added a pad lock to her bedroom door within an hour of moving in, demanding no one else enter unless she was there to supervise.

Jessa's mother had warned her that other's weird habits was just one of the experiences she would have to learn to live with in a share-house. That it would make her 'grow as a person' or whatever. Personally Jessa hated that sentiment because it was up there with believing everything happens for a reason which her grandmother used to say constantly. Or her other favourite: hardships were the water of life that polished rocks until they shine...or whatever. It had confused her as a child and now it just felt like a way to minimize a person's pain and make them feel bad for even bringing them up. In Jessa's opinion it was everyone's right to complain and gripe.

But it was still a pain to have to try and find exactly the right damn brand of chips.

'I hope the fact that girl's doing a psych degree helps her sort some of her shit out,' Jessa thought.

They were all doing their best to keep Elle happy because she hadn't been too sure about the party to begin with. Jessa had left her and Sam hooking up various speakers to a central music station while she did a 'supply run'. Although that had been *before* she realized that rather than a simple run-in-run-out situation, she had pretty much been sent on what equated to as a scavenger hunt or mission to discover the lost city of Atlantis.

"Choreos...Choreos," she muttered under her breath. "...I should have gotten a damn trolley." She had assumed a basket would do and was now trying to balance all the other chips, dips, drinks and bag of oranges of all things – Jessa had no idea why Tez had wanted those but he did. Lemons she could understand for shots, but *oranges*?! – and a tub of ice-cream for herself. No one else understood it, but Jessa found there was nothing tastier than dipping nacho chips into vanilla ice-cream. It even tasted good first thing in the morning, although she knew what her mother would say about *that* in terms of an appropriate breakfast. But she could have ice cream if she damn well wanted to and any damn time.

She thought she spotted the start of the word 'Che – ' on a packet of something on the very top shelf. She could only read half of the word because the packet had fallen on its side and was the last one in a box on the very uppermost shelf, well and truly out of her reach.

'Why the hell would they do that?' Jessa though irritably. Surely the number one purchasers of these chips would be teenagers and kids and there was absolutely no way they could reach them. She wasn't even that freakin' short and yet here she was, considering climbing the bottom shelf and wondering if it would be enough to hold her weight or not.

'There are other stores. 'I'll just get this stuff and then go to a service station. They'll probably cost three times as much but whatever, I'll pay. Or I'll just tell Elle they didn't have any – or she can come down and – '

A hand suddenly reached past, grabbing the packet and holding it out to her.

"Thanks!" Jessa said. "I hate how they put some stuff up so high. Don't they know not all of us bring a step ladder with us...?"

Jessa had been hoping to share a laugh with her would-be saviour but then she got a good look at him and stopped short.

He had backed away as soon as she'd taken the chips but was still a little uncomfortably close as she found herself face to face with his chest. He was thin, almost painfully so, about thirty, dark hair and one of those thick, full beards that was in right now. He was also incredibly pale, his eyes shiny but seemingly with no expression at all. In fact, he didn't even acknowledge her existence much less respond to her attempt at a conversation, something Jessa would have been thrown by anyway but even more so now. She unconsciously gripped the chip packet a little tighter, crushing the contents until the guy walked past her and back to his own trolley.

Now he was past her, Jessa didn't bother trying to cover her blatant staring. He was wearing long pants and check-button-up shirt – looking like her old high-school math teacher. He walked slightly hunched over either because he wasn't feeling well or maybe it was the constant positon of someone a little embarrassed by their height. She'd had a friend who did the same thing because she towered over everyone else so much. He had a slight shuffle to his step and was pushing his trolley as though it was piled high with groceries when really there were only a few items and a small child sitting in the front seat, happily kicking its feet out but otherwise quiet and content just gumming on a teething husk.

There was no resemblance between father and child that Jessa could see – the kid was chubby but that adorable chubby which would probably disappear once he started walking properly. The kid *was* wearing a blue romper with trains on it so she was leaning towards boy but of course the parents could be that type who dressed their daughter like this as some kind of statement to society. The father certainly looked the part of a hipster, minus the skinny jeans – but Jessa was willing to hedge her bets that she was admiring a little boy.

He had strawberry blond ringlets that looked gorgeous now but would no doubt cause him absolute hell in his school years if they didn't grow out and even the kid's rosy, chubby cheeks were perfect. If not for the excessive amounts of drool, he almost looked all set for a nappy commercial or Bonds romper ad. Of course Jessa had heard horror stories about babies when they were at the new-born-stage, the walking stage, the terrible twos, at school, and then of course, teenagers.

'I'm never having children,' Jessa thought with a shake of her head. Still, the kid was grinning at her with such reckless abandon that she couldn't help but grin back and even though she hadn't been successful the first time, she trailed after the man a few steps, ready to compliment him on his child – after all, was there any possible better way to get on a parent's good side than to praise their offspring? – but getting closer to him just gave her more things to be nervous about.

The man wasn't just pale but the complete opposite of healthy. His eyes had a blankness that made Jessa want to avoid him, possibly even duck to the end of the store completely and wait until she was sure he had left, just to be on the safe side. But unfortunately –

'Unfortunately part of being an adult is being responsible and concerned when you think someone might be in trouble,' an annoying little voice lectured her. Jessa wanted to ignore it and if she had still been at home living with her Mum than it's likely she would have. However she had been out on her own for a couple of months now and making such a big deal out of being mature and that meant not being one of *those* people who just kept moving rather than involving themselves in someone else's problems.

'Besides, he might just brush me off for being a worry-wart anyway.'

"Hey, are you okay?" she asked.

He peered at her as though she was either miles away or he usually wore glasses but had forgotten them.

"I didn't mean to interrupt your train of thought or whatever," Jessa said, struggling to come up with a polite way to ask this. "I just thought...um, you don't look too good and...I could, um...push your trolley for you while you go around the store? Or maybe you could call someone – your wife or...husband...or whatever – who can come and help you..." It felt like she might have been talking in Swahili for all the reaction she was getting.

"Seriously," she said, trying again. "I could bring the store-manager if – " She stopped when he suddenly grimaced and his hand shot up to his mouth in what was possibly the universal signal of a person about to be sick.

Jessa instantly backed away – actually she *leapt* away – in order to be out of the 'spill zone'. But all he did was double over, resting his head on the handle bar of the trolley, as though needing it to remain standing.

"My stomach," the man managed to gasp out. "It hurts." These were the first and last words he said as he dropped to the floor. It was surprisingly graceful and had no fanfare so it was like this was almost normal.

The little boy stared down at his father and then glanced her way, grinning again as though this was some kind of game.

He was a lot less comfortable with Jessa's next course of action though – yelling for help – and possibly it was the panic he picked up on too because his face crumbled and after a few seconds he was shrieking right along with her.

2

It didn't take long for someone to come running and feeling slightly melodramatic, Jessa pointed at the man on the floor.

"Call an ambulance! I think he's got – it might be – appendix!"

The stock-boy apparently wasn't allowed to have his phone with him while he was on the job and so he had done an almost comical back-pedal towards the maintenance area to get both it and the manager. Jessa sincerely hoped they would be older and therefore able to take control of this situation, especially the kid who was building himself up into quite a crescendo, his face almost purple.

"Hey, don't worry," Jessa said to him. "It's all going to be okay. You're Dad's just...not feeling well at the moment. But we're gonna get him some help, 'kay?"

Of course the child didn't give a damn about what she was saying and Jessa glanced around for another customer. Surely there had to be one – there was always a woman in the supermarket – usually a mother – who would know how to deal with a crying child.

But Jessa was alone and the longer and louder the poor boy wailed, the more she felt her own tension levels rising until she wanted to start crying right alongside him.

"Geez, is this what it's like to *have* one of you?!" she muttered under her breath as she reached out a hand to the baby, thinking just to stroke his head or give his arm a pat or something. However, the minute she put her hands near him, he instantly held his arms up and while Jessa hesitated, finally she lifted the child up.

He wasn't quite as heavy as she had anticipated considering his size and he seemed to fit quite perfectly against her hip, wrapping his chubby little arms around her and resting his head into the crook of her shoulder. "At least one of us seems to know what they're doing," she muttered, trying not to think about the drool and sticky little finger marks ending up on her shirt.

"What...happened?!" The stock boy was back and clearly unfit considering how out-of-breath he was from a small jog from the staff room and back. "The emergency chick...wants...to know," he added, in case his first question had come across as accusatory.

"I don't know. He didn't look very well and I came over to ask if he was okay – he said something about his stomach – then just dropped."

The store manager followed him at a much slower pace, partly because she was well-past middle aged and also because she was dragging along an over-sized first-aid-kit – oh, and had about five times as much body weight as her height and bones probably were meant to have.

"Do you know him," she asked Jessa. She was nowhere near as out of breath as the stock-boy, oddly.

"No," Jessa said. "He just helped me reach some chips and…"

The manager checked the man's pulse and tried to rouse him while the stock-boy 'danced' from foot to foot, not doing anything practical but seemingly unable to stop moving.

They all heard the sirens in the distance and the manager gruffly told the stock-boy to go out the front and direct them here.

"Is he going to be alright?" Jessa asked her in a hushed voice despite the fact there wasn't anyone nearby to overhear. It was like she was trying to spare the baby.

"Not sure. I've only done a basic first-aid courses. He's breathing though and his heart rate's racing but…"

Luckily she was saved from having to attempt a 'formal diagnosis' by the sound of the stock-boy chattering away, telling what he knew about the situation – which truth be told, wasn't much.

"I don't know – the guy just dropped. I mean, this chick started screaming – but by the time we got there he was down – there's no blood so I don't know if she did anything to him – but she coulda done, right? Should you get police back-up…?" He trailed off when he saw Jessa glaring at him, wilting under her gaze.

The ambulance officers weren't paying much attention anyway, their focus was solely on their patient. Jessa took a few steps back, not going far – she wanted to be ready to hand over the kid as soon as someone asked for it. He was being calm enough now, twiddling his fingers through her hair, but this was probably only temporary.

"Hey, so what's that about?" she asked him. "Doesn't your mother have long hair?"

"Mamma!" he grinned at her in response as though this was the punch line to some great joke. Jessa rolled her eyes, but was amused too. "Don't worry, we'll get you back to her as soon as possible. And your Dad's going to be okay too, you'll see."

He looked over her shoulder at the shelves, reaching for something.

"Uh-huh little guy, none of that." She grabbed his hand to hold it away but wasn't really paying attention as she heard a fuss coming from the direction of the medicos and looked over with alarm when she saw them pulling wires out of their bags and attaching them to the guy.

'Heart attack,' was what her mind immediately jumped to and she turned slightly so the kid couldn't see what was happening.

"No! Naughty – bad boy," she said, trying to wrestle the packet of popcorn away from him. The box had been gnawed on a little ('What the hell happened to the kid's husk?!') but he hadn't managed to actually break through the packaging and it only looked slightly worse for wear. Inwardly Jessa groaned though as she realized she might have to pay for it – and it wasn't even the good brand!

"Give me a break here kid, okay?" She didn't have time to hide the destruction because the manager was waddling towards her.

"Are you sure you don't know the man?" she asked.

"Ah, no."

"They're taking him to the hospital," she said, eyeing the baby and probably thinking the same thing Jessa was.

"So um, what do we do with this guy?" Jessa asked, bouncing him slightly on her hip.

"The man's not carrying a phone...yeah, I know," she added after seeing the look of disbelief on Jessa's face. "And no wallet either."

"What was he doing shopping?!"

"Don' know."

"Do they know what's wrong with him?"

"In their own words: it's not the ambo's job to diagnose." The manager stared at the kid with pursed lips for several seconds, as though weighing up her options. "I can't go with him," she said finally. "I supposed I could always send Ryan..."

"Ryan...?"

The manager jerked her head to indicate the stock-boy who was back to bouncing back and forth, still excited but in no way constructive.

"I don't know how he is with kids but..."

Jessa felt like she had known how this was going to end up all along but still tried to put up a token fight. "Shouldn't the police be called then?" she asked. "Isn't it *their* job to deal with...left behind?...kids?"

"It is. But it would probably be better if the father and the child stay together and they get called from the hospital...and I can't leave the store," she repeated. "I'm the only one rostered on for the rest of the day – even Ryan's only on for another hour. Otherwise..."

Jessa wasn't entirely sure how much of that was true – the rostered part maybe but more likely the manager didn't want to sit in a hospital waiting room for who knows how long, trying to entertain a kid no one knew anything about.

"He seems to like you," she added pointedly.

"But, my shopping...?" Jessa started to say but the manager was already waving her hand.

"We'll put it back for you and the next time you come in we'll give you a fifty-dollar voucher."

Jessa couldn't deny that her spirits rose slightly at the thought of that – for someone on a budget such as her, even a found two-dollar coin was enough to give her a thrill. And she *did* like the kid and felt bad for the father who was no doubt having a far worse day than she was. It would be good for her karma too and –

"And who knows, I might end up being your favourite Aunt Jessa or something," she murmured to the kid after it was decided it would be easier if she just rode in the ambulance with everyone else rather than deal with baby-seats or trying to figure out how to drive the guy's van.

She was hoping someone would give her a lift afterwards considering she was leaving her ride behind – or maybe she could just let Tez know he had to figure out a way to get his car from the supermarket – after all, they were going to have to go back for their munchies anyway.

Chapter Two –

1

Jessa had never ridden in an ambulance before so for her it was an adventure to be racing along with the sirens wailing and the lights flashing. It wasn't lost on her that it couldn't be a good sign that the professionals thought the guy's condition was bad enough to warrant all the bells and whistles and she held the kid just that little bit closer even.

"Don't worry," she found herself murmuring to the kid. "It will work out." She might as well have been talking to herself though as she glanced down and realized the kid was lazing on her shoulder. 'Must be nice to be young and able to sleep through *any*thing.'

2

Of course, if the kid had been older then he would have been able to help out with telling them a phone number or some other personal details that most people take for granted in emergency situations when someone important asks.

"I don't know," Jessa said again for what felt like the tenth time in a row. "I don't know anything at all about these people."

"All we need is a last name and then we can look him up in the system," the receptionist at the desk continued, apparently choosing to ignore Jessa's continued pleas of ignorance.

"I just met him at the store – in fact I *didn't* even meet him! He reached for some chips I couldn't and then fell down!"

"You didn't ask him his name?"

"Why the hell would I? – he was just some guy!" Jessa wondered if there was just some part of this she wasn't getting considering the way the woman was looking at her with a raised eyebrow. "What do you think is going on here?" she asked finally.

"Come on, a young thing like you – hanging out with a family man...it doesn't take a genius."

Jessa mouth dropped open. "You think I'm having an *affair* with the guy?! And what, he brought his child along for our little rendezvous?!"

The receptionist continued with her smug, knowing look.

"I think I'll just wait for the police," Jessa said through gritted teeth, afraid of what she might add if continued this conversation.

"You do that. But – "

3

Jessa hadn't waited to hear the rest, going back to the waiting room seats and purposefully picking one with its back to the receptionist. This left her staring at a black glass window that normally might have shown a scenic view of the outside car-park but because the sun was setting, the vista was changing to just her own reflection. Jessa wasn't interested in seeing how agitated she looked and so concentrated on the kid.

She hadn't quite reached the point where she wished she had never gotten involved with any of this yet, but wasn't far from it. The minute they had arrived at the hospital – taking longer than she expected because there had been a great deal of cars on the road all trying to get to the hospital too – the guy had immediately been taken through the electronic doors that kept the waiting room separate from the actual medical part of the ER. With hindsight Jessa realized she should have kept up but she had tried to stay out of everyone's way and had been stuck outside ever since.

In their defence, the hospital staff did seem to be run off their feet – well, with the exception of the bitchy, conspiracy theory receptionist who was quite possibly behind the desk playing solitaire for all Jessa knew. Ambulance after ambulance had been pulling into the docking bay around the front, rushed through with no one being able to stop and talk to Jessa beyond directing her to the receptionist who was giving her so much grief.

Jessa's only hope was that the receptionist might be on shift just like everyone else at the hospital, at which point someone new would arrived, hopefully a little more helpful.

"Of course it's not like they could be any less, right big guy?" Jessa asked the kid, pausing only long enough to glance at the doors opening again, the patient mostly covered by a blanket – although there was an 'interesting' stain near one of his legs.

"It's kind of crazy here today, isn't it? Cranky people and insane ladies who really have no idea what's going on – and even if they did, it sure as hell wouldn't be any of their damn business, right?" The kid gurgled at her and Jessa guessed it had something to do with the sing-song way she was speaking that was keeping him so amused.

She felt her stomach roll queasily from hunger. She had been hungry even before going on her little snack run but was wary about getting something from the vending machine because she knew the minute the kid saw her with food, regardless of how hungry he might not be himself, he would automatically hold out his little hand for some.

"And *that* would open up a whole new can of worms, wouldn't it kid?" she said.

Luckily she had been able to ignore her hunger pains so far due to the smell coming from the kid that made it very, very obvious he needed a nappy-change – and not only had she never changed a nappy before but the father hadn't had a nappy bag with him or any kind of bag at all really – and the thought of one hadn't occurred to Jessa until much, much later.

"Live and learn, eh kid?"

Jessa supposed she could have gone and bought some nappies but the hospital gift shop hadn't stocked that kind of thing and the person behind the counter had directed her to a shopping centre that was supposedly "not too far away". Jessa was afraid of leaving though and so after double-checking the receptionist looked distracted, she murmured, "Okay kid, I have a naughty idea. Now I don't want to encourage this but desperate times, call for desperate measures."

Acting casual, Jessa stood up and strolled in the direction of the elevators, standing exposed for a few minutes while waiting for the doors to open and once inside, let out her breath. She had hoped the floors would be labelled, designations next-to the buttons to let people know what speciality was on which floor. She hadn't been looking forward to having to traverse the entire hospital searching for the maternity ward and luckily in bold, easy to read black and white there had been – OBSTETRICS, *level 5*.

"Five – my lucky number," she said, deciding to take it as an omen. The doors had opened onto a ward that had seemed far more bustling and crazy than the waiting room and while this should have made things harder because it there were far more people around to notice her, because it was so chaotic Jessa was able to slip by with very little grief at all. It also didn't hurt that she was carrying a baby which meant she seemed to almost 'fit in' with people assuming she was there with her own sick child.

'Must be a full moon,' Jessa thought, not really paying too much attention to the fact that many of the wards had people propped on beds up against the walls and quite often, not looking even remotely like they belonged on this particular floor.

Jessa was more focussed on her search for a supply trolley. She knew from articles and movies that mothers-to-be were meant to 'pack a bag' when they headed to the hospital – it was always one of the lines when people were rushing out the door: "Honey, don't forget to grab the bag!" – but a hospital had to keep some supplies on hand for emergencies, didn't they?

Sure enough, after a few laps, Jessa found a supply closet and even though she had never felt more like a criminal in her life, she raided it.

The majority of the supplies were geared towards newborns and Jessa had to search for the biggest size (temporarily amusing herself with the image of finding the seniors section of the hospital instead and seeing if she could snag a few adult diapers) however eventually she found some that would work and also, a collection of things she grabbed just-in-case. Lotions and powders – even bottles and formula that she felt really, really bad about appropriating but figured she could always donate them to a women's shelter or something when the kid's *real* mother showed up.

There was a canvas bag hospitals always seemed to have which she turned inside out to hide the logo and then headed for the elevators again.

4

"Well that was an adventure, wasn't it?" Jessa said to the baby as they returned from the bathroom and sat back down. She was feeling tired and like what she had just done should have been easy but for some reason had been an ordeal. She had assumed it would be disgusting but she hadn't quite anticipated changing a nappy would be so confusing.

"It also didn't help that you put up such a fuss," she said. "If it had been me I would have been *overjoyed* at the prospect of getting rid of that full, stinky nappy!"

The kid rested his head on her shoulder again, apparently as exhausted as she was. For once he wasn't responding to her cheery comments and in fact, his face crumbled in on itself again and she recognized this as meaning he was about to start wailing again.

"Oh come on, kid! Give me a break here – I don't know what you want! – haven't we already established this?"

In response he tried to ham his whole fist in his mouth and suck. Jessa at first assumed it was the whole teeth thing again but then it occurred to her that she was hungry too and babies were supposed to eat every few hours or something.

"Damn it!" she cursed. "Whose bright idea was this in the first place?! I should have told that damn manager no!" Even though she hadn't wanted to call her mother – along with her whole 'good karma' image had been the pleasure she would feel when she told her about this and how she had handled it all on her own and kept her cool and did all the right things and acted like an adult. All that good stuff parents rarely believed their children were capable of without some solid proof. Now though, Jessa was ready to throw in the towel, admit defeat and call in the reserves.

She passed a vending machine on her way out, staring at all the "goodies" on display and while she probably could have made some joke about the availability of 'healthy food choices' at a hospital, she was just too hungry.

"Besides, one packet of potato chips and a chocolate bar isn't going to kill us, is it?"

The kid gurgled in response and Jessa wasn't sure if he recognized the packaging or had just assumed that since she had finally gotten around to changing his nappy, she was now going to get around to supplying him with food to refill it again. Either way, he had started to drool excessively again and kick his legs.

"Okay then. How 'bout we go with... some plain potato chips – can't go wrong with them, can we? And...choc-chip cookie? What do you think?"

More vigorous leg kicking.

"What's this then?" she asked. "Do you know the words choc-chip? Well that's a sign."

5

Jessa wasn't all that surprised when her mother didn't immediately text back. Technology just wasn't her mother's expertise and it could potentially be a full hour before a) her mother realized why her phone had made that strange sound, b) figured out how to read it and then c) responded.

"And the party's probably in full swing now," she muttered, not even looking up as three ambulances arrived all at once, tyres screeching and drivers abusing each other over who's patient was more critical and who's driving skills were less adequate. Jessa was too busy feeling sorry for herself that no one in the share house had noticed her absence or bothered to send her a text to find out where she was or what was holding her up. "You'd at least think they'd care about their lack of food."

Jessa was vaguely interested as *these* patients came shuffling in holding bloody towels to their heads or sides. The group looked like they had been part of a bar-room brawl or mob scene, but the medicos were mentioning how they had all come from different parts of town, complaining within earshot as they waited for their paperwork to be processed.

"Why the fuck are we being sent out to Westin and Adelphi? Isn't that Carl's and Devo's route?"

"They're overrun with calls from Havenport."

"*Havenport*?! What the hell are they doing all the way out there?!"

"Some kind of music festival got out of hand or something. So many casualties they can't keep up."

"What kinds of casualties – overdose rush?"

"Nah, I don't think so."

"Did a stage collapse?"

"No. They were reporting that there was a mob going after people – attacking everyone in sight."

"Chemically induced?"

"Maybe. They've been trying to sedate and restrain people for hours. Sam and Jonesy – have you met him yet? – he's new. They were the first on the scene and started carting the most serious cases out of there but never made it to the hospital."

"Where are *they*?"

"No one knows! They're probably broken down somewhere – or even got lost – they were out in the boonies after all. But then no one can understand why they haven't used their radio to call for help."

"Maybe that's broken too?"

"We're supposed to check all of our equipment before we leave the station – and you know Sam, she has checklists for her checklists."

"Do you think they ran into trouble?"

"I hope not. But no one can go and check yet because we're all so swamped!"

"It doesn't make any difference anyway," a new receptionist interrupted and in her joy at discovering it was no longer the original, unhelpful one, Jessa didn't really pay attention to what was being said. "You can't bring any more patients here – I just got word from up high. We're full to capacity."

"What are you talking about – ?"

"And where are we supposed to take these people – ?!"

"Evermeer has already refused to take any more as well!"

"Hey, don't shoot the messenger guys," she said, holding her hands up in surrender. "I'm only reporting what I've been told."

"But it's going crazy out there for some reason – what are we supposed to do?!"

"Excuse me," Jessa interrupted.

"I know you have already probably had a very long wait but we're a little overwhelmed at the moment – "

"No, it's not that. I'm here because I was out shopping and this guy, he..."

Chapter Three –

1

"Are you sure you don't want me to take the baby?" Denny the receptionist asked.

"No, I've got him."

"Really, we have cots set up – they're normally in the paediatric ward, but I'm sure I could commandeer one. And then you wouldn't have to – "

"No – I'd really prefer he stay with me. I know I'm probably just being silly but I feel like he's my responsibility and I don't want anything to happen on my watch."

"However you want," Denny said with a shrug.

The kid was fast asleep in her arms, blissfully ignoring all the craziness that was the 'behind the doors' of the emergency room.

Jessa had *some* idea of the chaos considering what everyone had been saying but she hadn't thought it would be *this* crazy. Medical personnel rushed back and forth, patients screamed in pain and various equipment either beeped loudly or sent out siren wails indicating something was very, very wrong.

"Is it always like this?" Jessa asked, stunned.

"It can get a little crazy sometimes," Denny answered. However even *she* seemed a little taken aback by some of the bedlam and after directing Jessa to a cubicle near the back, walked over to the nurse's station, talking rapidly to what looked like an already harried nurse.

"You ready to see Dadda?" Jessa asked the kid, walking away. "I bet he can't wait to see you!"

Denny hadn't been able to give her an update on the father's condition – mainly because Jessa hadn't been able to give her a name to check. However, the fact he was a 'John Doe' had still helped because only five had been admitted that day and the original medicos had left a note on the chart about a child and the 'good samaritan' waiting outside.

She wasn't quite sure what was going to be achieved by being closer to the guy considering he was still unconscious but who knows, maybe it would be one of those miracles where the presence of his child or the sound of the kid's cry would magically break through his coma. Jessa knew shit like this probably only happened in the movies but she was also almost delirious with boredom and exhaustion and if this happened then maybe she would then be able to convince herself that the guy was awake enough to give her the okay to go home – taking the kid with her of course. She could then come back again in the morning after everyone had a decent night's sleep.

This idea had occurred to her before – many times in fact – but it was always drowned out by another side which argued this would constitute as kidnapping and it was entirely possible that rather than walk into the hospital the next morning to welcoming people so grateful she had helped them out and taken such good care of their son, it would be to hysterical parents and a police arrest!

'But seriously, all the guy did was reach for some chips for me – does that really mean I'm forced to adopt you?" She hesitated at the curtain, obviously unable to knock but unsure of what was happening on the other side.

"Ah, hello?" she said. "My name is Jessa...and I'm not sure if you remember me but...but you're not even conscious anyway. Great. Just great."

And more than that, he didn't look any better either. His complexion was still an ugly grey colour and his thin build seemed even more extreme lying in a hospital bed. In fact, if anything the poor guy looked like he was dying.

She looked over her shoulder at the bustling emergency room and tried to get a nurse's attention. This was obviously the kind of situation where the squeakiest wheels were going to get the oil – specifically those currently screaming and complaining the loudest – but everyone looked completely run off their feet.

Jessa carefully touched the man's cheek, the red colour indicating a fever but his skin *actually* felt cold and like he should have been shivering with the chills. She leant her face down close to him or as close as she could get while still trying to balance a baby on her hip. From this angle she was able to see his eyes were slightly open and like he might have been watching her.

"Don't worry pal, I'm going to go find a nurse and make sure they still know you're here and look after you..." she said automatically, trailing off when she saw his eyes swivel slightly towards her even as he stopped breathing. Even though it hurt her back a little to stay hunched over at such a strange position, she stayed exactly where she was, with one ear practically to his chest, almost *willing* it to rise.

Jessa wanted to call out for help but was afraid to move in case she missed the sign that he was still alive. She was sure it had to happen soon because there was no way he was dead...no way...no chance...

"Um...nurse?" she started to say, just as he suddenly lunged for her.

Chapter Four –

1

Jessa had never been in a fight in her life and never thought she would. She wasn't the type who lost her temper or did anything other than use her words and so because of all of this, she was surprised by her reaction to the man grabbing her.

It was as though one moment she had been all about saving him – and the next she had been thrashing against him, pushing and punching for all she was worth, yelling at him to "Stop!" and let her go – let her go right *now*! He didn't take much notice and just continued to use one hand around her neck to pull her in closer and closer to his face.

Jessa didn't know his intention – whether it was to tell her something private or important, or even to kiss her which seemed possible the way he kept opening and closing his mouth – but it was *not* happening.

She heard a strange sound coming from his chest and realized he was actually growling at her and she allowed the kid to drop to the floor so he fell rather abruptly as she continued trying to fight off his father.

He was close enough how that she could feel the gust of his mouth opening and closing, hovering just below hers, their lips almost touching. His eyes had opened completely but while he might have been looking at her, it was like he was seeing *through* her.

"Let me go!" Jessa repeated, trying to push him away but succeeding in doing nothing but keeping him from gaining across those last few inches as he got a firmer grip on her hair. She kept waiting for someone to come help – but it was the kid finally getting over his shock of being dumped to the floor and starting to scream which worked.

The sound of his pain and fear was enough to add to her own and power her aggression. She pushed against him again, although this time not with the aim of breaking free but simply to bring her arms up, one locking under his chin and the other reaching for his face. The guy reacted by rolling her, taking them both off the bed and pushing her to the floor so he was on top. Without thinking Jessa pushed again, grinding her thumb directly in his eye.

She expected an instantaneous reaction but the only thing she achieved was for his head to tilt slightly more in that direction as a result of her pressure. She pushed harder to demonstrate she really meant business and that he was about to lose an eye but again, he only leaned more on that side.

"I *will* hurt you," she cried before *really* digging her finger in.

She was momentarily distracted by just how easy it was. The fleshy orb popped under her finger almost right away and with surprising satisfaction. If she viewed it scientifically and detached she could note the warm sensation, that it was slightly gooey but very little blood. That her finger kept going until it was buried almost up to her third knuckle and she finally felt the resistance of what might have possibly been the skull.

Again she expected screaming and his grip *did* loosen enough for her to duck away – but if anything, he just seemed perplexed that one of his eyes was gone, throwing his balance off and causing him to slide back. Jessa pushed away from the bed, her attention solely on the man who had one hand vaguely up to his eye but otherwise looking at something over her shoulder. It was almost like he had forgotten about her. But that didn't make any sense –

She crab walked backwards a few steps, putting her in the path of a nurse who tripped over Jessa, almost falling before spinning around to yell at her, "What the hell are you doing – look where you're going!"

Jessa opened her mouth and pointed at the father but no sound would come out. Not that it mattered since the nurse was suddenly and viciously wrestled to the ground by another patient.

The nurse didn't scream when she was taken down – she was too surprised – or at least that was Jessa's impression. And unlike Jessa, she was *not* able to get her hands up in time and the patient went straight for her throat, burrowing into it like an overzealous vampire.

Jessa heard more screams behind her and scrambled back towards the bed on her hands and knees. She ducked under the corner of it even though it wasn't much of a shield thanks to all the mechanics underneath it, but still provided the illusion of safety as she watched the emergence of hell around her.

Chapter Five –

1

Jessa hadn't paid attention to any of the other patients before so it was like she was seeing them for the first time.

An incredibly old lady with her wrist plastered and what looked like a fairly nasty cut to her forehead had backed a nurse into a corner, her hands hooked into claws. The nurse was holding her hands out in front of her as though trying to ward her off but otherwise looking completely unsure of what else to do. Her nose was already bleeding so this wasn't the first time the octarian had come after the poor woman – and the nurse was going to be yelling for help for a while as everyone else was just as preoccupied.

There was the patient who looked like he had been in a motorcycle accident, secured to one of those body boards complete with neck brace. This was the one thing saving his doctor because he had only managed to get himself partially free and so was being hampered by the overly large contraption attached to his head. Jessa guessed in this type of situation, medical staff would have been encouraging the guy to get back in bed – probably no doubt with physical force in necessary, but the doctor was staring at him in wonder even as she cradled what looked like a broken arm against her chest.

Another doctor was batting at a different male patient with what looked like an IPAD. This patient was possibly in the morbidly obese category and had likely been at the hospital with chest pains if his size had anything to do with it. His button up shirt had been opened and there were several wires hanging down on his waist, forgotten. His stomach fat wobbled, his complexion was the same odd, grey colour that the father's had been. The fat man currently had his face buried in the abdomen of a nurse that had been helping him, tearing and ripping at the flesh even as she continued to scream as the other doctor tried to help. The doctor had already created a large crack in the device and was screaming guttural noises and calling the patient every curse word under the sun to get him to stop but was going unnoticed by the fat man.

There were two party revellers – possibly from the rave the medicos had been talking about – wearing bright coloured clothing, glow stick bracelets and an assortment of party-tent stamps on their wrists and lower arms. They had both been brought in on stretchers, one of them was still laid-out peacefully while her friend looked like she was having a seizure.

Jessa wasn't sure what had gone on at the rave but the chick had been attacked with a glass bottle, said implement now lodged in her face, possibly already broken even before it had been turned into the weapon almost taking out her eye. There were two deep gashes both above and below it, the skin torn away with such force that it was now flapping down almost to her mouth. It made her look like she was crying bloody tears as she suddenly reached for her unconscious friend, thwarted temporarily by a blood-pressure cuff still attached to one arm and a nurse who was doing her best to put her body between the patients, not realizing the danger. Then the unconscious girl's hand starting to twitch and shake too.

There were two nurses in the corner, holding onto each other and watching with disbelief, screaming out a warning to their comrade but to no avail.

A pregnant woman in a wheel-chair, either hyper-ventilating and screaming due to onset labour or because currently her husband was being set upon by two patients and what now looked like a nurse who had been attacked herself and was now reacting in much the same way as the crazy patients.

There was a little girl by some doors, about five or six years old, her face tear-streaked as she wailed for her Mummy, while at the same time backing away. Before Jessa could do anything to help, one of the crazy ones spotted her and made a dive for her. By luck she managed to dodge away and then ran screaming, deeper into the hospital even as the crazy gave chase.

Jessa probably would have continued watching mindlessly except there was a wail behind her and she remembered the danger *she* was in.

2

The fact that the crazies had the attention span of a fruit-fly had worked in her favour in that the father had forgotten all about her and instead gone after the one thing now making the most noise – the kid.

Like most of the other patients the Dad had gotten caught up in the various tubes and wires that had been attached to monitor his health – most of which were screaming and beeping now – which had delayed him for several moments, saving the child. He had one hand hooked onto the kid's legs though, intent on pulling the kid the rest of the way to him.

Jessa stood over the man and then brought her foot down as hard as she could on his lower back. She felt something snap and just like that, he legs stopped twitching. If this had been a normal situation than Jessa guessed this now would have been the moment when he would have howled about the pain and she would have had to start worrying about things such as crippling a man and leaving him wheel-chair bound for life.

Instead though, he only seemed to glance down, confused as to why his legs were no longer enabling him to crawl towards the thing making all the noise and rip it to pieces.

Jessa didn't waste any extra time trying to inflict more damage. She grabbed the kid's leg herself, sliding him along the floor towards her and then scooping him up in one smooth move. The kid's arms instantly went around her neck, almost in a choking bind as he screamed in her ear but this was secondary as Jessa swung around to get away.

Many of the fights were still going on – most of those under attack seemed to be losing Jessa noted – but Jessa *really* didn't want to be around when the screaming thing in front of them became less interesting then the screaming, wriggling thing making all the noise over there. So she buried the child's face in her shoulder and kicked her foot out when someone tried to grab her ankle – for assistance or to attack she didn't know – and wasn't about to wait around to find out.

She stopped to help no one else, ignoring all the pleas and just kept her eye on the door and then, into the waiting room.

3

She fled out into the night, completely alone and all seemingly peaceful and quiet. The kid quietened some, possibly because she had been holding him so tight it had become a comfort. There was a faint breeze and Jessa found herself halting to watch the leaves rustling in a tree, as though it was of great importance – until she remember just how screwed she was.

Tez's car was still in the supermarket car-park and it wasn't like she could catch the bus at this time of night. Walking would take forever – and she also really didn't think it would be particularly safe tonight. She had merely wanted to get away from the hospital ward and now...

"Is this real?" she wondered aloud and the sound of her own voice didn't make her feel any better or act as proof that this wasn't a crazy hallucination her tired mind had come up with. And because of that, she was able to do what she did next and not allow her law-abiding side to argue.

She stole a car.

Not that it had been all that difficult – the car had been it had been practically *begging* someone to take it. Or at least that was the spin she was putting on it rather than speculate about why someone to drive up to the hospital, manage to get as far as the carpark and park with two wheels on the curb and the other two in the landscaped garden, and abandoning it with the keys in the ignition. The driver's side door had even been wide open, as though they had either been pulled through and out – or had chased something on foot. There was absolutely no sign of anybody now though, the night cool and calm.

She laid the kid out on the backseat with the middle seatbelt wrapped around his body – no doubt not going to do much if they *were* in a crash but at least making her feel better and like she was doing the 'right thing' to look after the kid.

She turned the ignition and sent out a quick thank-you to her mother who had demanded Jessa learn how to drive a stick shift despite all of Jessa's complaints that she had an auto and that no one really drove a stick shift anymore.

"You were right as always Mum," she murmured as she reminded herself which pedal was which and flooded the car only twice as she slowed down at the turn to join the other traffic.

She drove past a gas station that had one car already driven through the front windows, smashing them to all hell, and two more out by the pumps, each missing their drivers and the doors once again left wide open. There was no sign of any people although Jessa thought she might have seen movement inside the store. Jessa drove on though, unable to fight the feeling that she had somehow fallen into an episode of the Twilight Zone.

Chapter Six –

1

Jessa wasn't entirely sure what happened to her in the ensuing few hours. She of course remembered driving and seeing various acts she had never thought she would witness in her lifetime. Bodies lying randomly in the street with no one coming to help them; people walking around dazed, with blood and wounds that looked really quite horrific and in some cases, had Jessa wondering how on earth they were still standing, much less walking around.

Either through luck or muscle memory, she found her way to her share house, not bothering going for her own car just yet and simply wanting to get behind locked doors.

The house was on a quiet street and from the outside it looked like nothing was wrong with the world. It was a two story town-house without much of a front or back yard which suited a group of studying twenty-somethings. After all it was wonder enough if someone decided to do a load of laundry or threw out something in the fridge when it had mould on it. It was five bedroom – two of which probably weren't technically meant to be classed as bedrooms, one more likely was a study and the other the equivalent of a study nook that barely even fit a single bed, however that particular room wasn't Jessa's, so she hadn't cared so much. Besides, Tez paid significantly less than the rest of them.

Jessa stared at the front of the house for several minutes, trying to understand what she was feeling. It now felt like a dream but all she had to do was grip the unfamiliar steering wheel or glance in the back at the kid who was sound asleep, for proof enough of her current reality.

2

Jessa felt so out of sorts that she almost knocked on the front door, as if she needed permission to come in. At that time of the morning after a rager of a party she seriously doubted anyone would have bothered to answer – even if she had been there with a siren though.

Plus, it was unlocked.

'Elle is going to have a fit when she finds out,' Jessa thought but with no particular emotion. Then again, maybe the guys had finally found a way to get her to loosen up considering she was face down on the couch in just a bra and high-waisted jeans, looking every bit the hard-partying university co-ed she had sworn up and down she wasn't and never would be.

She heard heavy footsteps coming down the stairs and turned that way.

"Jessa?!" Sam said. "Geez, where have you been?! You missed one EP-IC party last night! We even..."

Jessa had been standing with her side to him as he came down and now she swung around completely, revealing the kid who blinked at this new stranger with the sticking-up hair.

"Ahh, didn't we send you out for some chips and stuff? What are you doing with...?"

Jessa didn't even bother to open her mouth. She just felt so confused. Her one goal had been to get home and now she was here, she didn't know what to do next.

"Jessa?" a blearily voice called from the couch. "Do you have my Choroes?"

"Ah...no. But she does have a kid."

"A...what?!"

Jessa headed to the kitchen hoping maybe coffee would help. The kid seemed to recognize this particular room's purpose and he instantly began drooling and grizzling. Jessa realized she had the same exact problem as in the hospital – what on earth was she supposed to feed the kid from here? Finally she poured a bowl of cereal from the cupboard and put it in front of him dry. It was some kind of chocolate variety

Tez favoured but the kid seemed to be okay with it and started chowing down, grinning and happy as his pudgy fist waved back and forth.

'You have no idea I might have seriously maimed, if not outright killed your father last night, do you?'

Of course he didn't and Jessa too was doing everything she could to block it out too.

Sam and Elle followed her into the kitchen, Sam glancing at the kid who Jessa had set on the floor, still in her field of vision.

"Jessa...?" he said. "Jess, where did you get the kid?"

"The supermarket."

"...where are its parents?"

"...I don't...his mother never...but his Dad – I didn't mean to...he was..."

"Call the police," Elle advised from the hall way, sleep still partially in her eyes but otherwise coming back to herself.

"I don't think they will care," Jessa muttered. "Keep an eye on him for a sec, yeah?" she said to Sam before heading upstairs.

Elle had gone for the phone and was just starting to complain about people not paying the bill because it wasn't working as Sam called back that he didn't know anything about kids and what was he supposed to do if it started crying?!

Chapter Seven –

1

Jessa slung her backpack over her shoulder, sure she had packed all the wrong things. Clothes – her warmest ones – money (not that she had a whole lot beyond the emergency fifty her mother had given her when she had moved out) and then raided the bathroom cupboard for medical supplies. The most 'useful' things available were band aids and Panadol.

'I should have raided the hospital while I was there,' she thought. But of course this was a completely ridiculous notion because she had only been thinking of getting away.

While walking through the house she had noticed several party-goers, asleep in various positions and places, wondering if she should wake them up and warn them.

She had lost several minutes staring into Tez's room, him still fast asleep with a girl sleeping comfortably under each arm and a single sheet barely covering their modesty considering it was so threadbare it was borderline transparent. Jessa was caught half-way between thinking they all looked so peaceful – just like the other ones had, before they had changed – and how easy it would be for one of those crazy ones to get in here and just kill them all while they slept –

In fact she could picture it with such perfect detail and clarity that she glanced down the hall, half-expecting to see them coming – those girls with the stamps on their wrists, the old lady with the wires still attached and trailing – or even that father-to-be, having already attacked his wife and now looking for a little 'dessert'.

There was no one there though and Jessa forced herself to get moving again.

By the time she got back to the kitchen Elle had stopped her gripping about the phone bill as she was too busy pressing all the buttons on her mobile phone.

"It doesn't make any sense," she said. "Emergency numbers *have* to go through no matter what. Even if you have no credit – it's a law put through a couple of years ago!"

"At least you can't blame us for *that* phone not working," Sam muttered. Then louder, "Do you have battery power?" He wasn't really paying attention as he bounced the kid gently up and down on his knee while he gurgled and cooed.

"Yes," Elle said. "I'm not a complete moron – Jessa, how are you doing? Are you feeling better! Are you well?"

Jessa's brow furrowed as she tried to figure out what Elle's game was *now* even as she went to kitchen cupboards.

"You maybe wanna tell us what's going on with you? – hey, those are mine!"

Not wanting to get into it, Jessa dutifully put the rice crackers back.

"Seriously Jessa," Sam said from the table. "You're starting to freak us out a bit. What's happened?"

"Things have gone bad out there," she said finally.

"...well that's nice and...vague," Elle said dryly. "Do you maybe want to elaborate?"

Jessa glared at her. "*Bad* as in bad. Bad as in hell. As in gone to shit. As in people are going crazy for no reason and attacking each other."

"And the kid is...?" Sam asked.

"I found him."

"His parents?"

"Gone."

This resulted in another exchanged look between Elle and Sam which Jessa ignored, looking in the fridge and trying to remember of cheese could survive outside of a cool environment. Jessa couldn't even remember if cheese was something that could be given to kids and she glared at the phone on the wall, wishing desperately to talk to her mother.

"What are you doing anyway?"

"I'm going home."

"Huh?"

"There's no people there and my mother and – and..."

"And what you're just going to leave the kid here with us?!"

"And what's with that weird car out the front? What happened to Tez's car?"

Jessa's head hurt as she held three packets of two-minute noodles – they were Sam's so Elle couldn't say anything about the theft although she very much looked like she wanted to. Jessa waited for Sam to kick up a fuss but he was keeping quiet and just watching her passively. Maybe it was his quiet contemplation that did it or maybe even the way he was just so calmly playing with the kid. But either way, she finally stopped and told them the full story.

2

"So I killed him," she finished.

"You don't know that for sure," Elle said quickly much to Jessa's surprise. Out of all of them she had thought Elle would be the one to be the most horrified – until she took a closer look at her face and realized Elle didn't believe her.

"What about you?" she asked Sam. "Do you think I've lost my mind?"

"That all depends, I guess."

"On what?"

"On what you were watching on TV last night?"

"You think I dreamt it?" Jessa's voice was neutral – not because she didn't care, but because she couldn't believe they were being so quick to dismiss her.

"Jessa..."

"Why do you think I'm crazy exactly? It's not like I walk around trying to balance a pineapple on my head and say it's for my end-of-year thesis like Tez does. Or lock myself in my room like I'm Harold Holt minus the billions. *That's* Elle!"

"Hey!"

"Or – "

"Jessa," Sam interrupted, trying to be patient. "Just look at this from *our* perspective."

Part of the problem was, she could. They were just going to have to find out the danger for themselves – which apparently they were going to as they all hear the screams outside.

It wasn't necessarily completely out of the ordinary – they had neighbours with small children and teenage girls who liked to squeal and let out impressive shrieks that might potentially cause a person to come running when truthfully the only serious thing happening was their sister had taken their hairbrush or a brother had thought it would be hilarious to put an ice-cube down the back of their shirts.

This scream however, was different.

It sounded like someone absolutely terrified and in pain. Elle's head snapped instantly towards the noise and even Sam glanced up from tickling the kid's foot.

"What was that?" Elle asked.

Jessa said nothing but merely picked the kid up.

Elle moved towards the front room – maybe to look out the window. Jessa didn't need to look – she'd already seen it all – and besides, she was having a feeling that she was forgetting something. It was on the very tip of her tongue – something important she had noticed when she had first walked through the unlocked front door –

And then left it wide open behind her.

Chapter Eight –

1

Because of the layout of the house Elle had to walk into the living room and then around a corner in order to see the front door. Jessa on the other hand, only had to walk into the hall to find herself face to face with it.

Maybe it didn't automatically go for her because she had stood completely still, frozen in shock and fear. Elle was walking towards it though and then held out her otherwise useless mobile phone like a sacrifice.

It had been the businessman father from three doors down. He was married with two school-aged kids, sharing the school drop-off duties with his wife. Jessa didn't know what he did for a living beyond that he wore a suit everyday – including Saturday more often than not – and seemed like a fairly grim man, although always well-groomed.

He certainly wasn't that way today as it looked like he had gone to collect the newspaper from his lawn and hadn't gotten any further. He was wearing a dressing gown, flapping open to reveal his spotted pj bottom's underneath and a singlet that might have previously been white but was now covered in grass stains and blood that might have been from his own gushing nose or from whoever he had attacked on his way to finding the front door to their particular house open.

He had rounded on Elle first and she rather ridiculously threw her phone at him, with the small mechanical device bouncing harmlessly off his shoulder. Rather than run away Elle stood there screaming as he speared her to the floor, biting at her hands when she tried to bat him away.

Jessa wasn't sure if she screamed too – it felt like she had – but it didn't matter because Sam had already noticed something she hadn't: the group of other crazies who had been wandering outside on the street, now drawn by Elle's screams.

"Out the back," he said suddenly.

"What about the others – ?" Jessa had started to say as she heard the sounds of them coming down the stairs to find out what the problem was.

Unlucky for him it was Tez first, followed closely by one of his bed-mates, the second one either able to sleep through anything, or taking their sweet time because they were hungover. The chick on the stairs screamed as Jessa was silently moved back by Sam, pausing only briefly to grab her bag of goodies as she heard a large crash from behind her. Tez now lying on the floor, his jaw at a strange angle like it had become unhinged from where it should have been, one ear looking partially ripped off and at least his arm broken was a result of his fall or push over the railings. His eyes were open and he was staring straight ahead but with a glassiness to them.

She wanted to turn away from this *thing* who had been her friend only a few minutes earlier – fun and amusing, with un-paramounted luck when it came to charming the opposite sex – but she needed to witness the change in his eyes.

Later when she had a calm moment to examine the incident, she realized it actually had nothing to do with his eyes at all. They had stayed blank and empty as he struggled to roll over and pull himself along on the carpet to get to her.

"Jessa, we need to go." Sam gave her a much harsher shove that almost took her off her feet. "Right now!"

"Where are we going?" she asked Sam as he dragged her towards the back door.

"...my family," Sam said, almost off-the-cuff. "They don't live too far away from here...well, they do – but only far enough away to not be having this happen around them."

"How can you be sure?"

By now they had made it out the door and down the back steps Jessa's legs feeling rubbery and weak and like they were going to collapse at any minute. They both froze at the sound of another scream – the share house next door. Jessa thought she saw movement in the window of the second story bathroom but tripped over her own feet and so only heard the glass break before a body landed in front of them.

The young woman was dressed only in pretty, frilly lingerie that Jessa had never seen any woman wear outside of movies and what teenage boys thought girls wore to bed. Clearly she had been another one who had not been prepared for this particular wake-up call and had been literally dragged out of bed. She whimpered slightly and now it was *Jessa's* turn to stop Sam and drag him away before he could get close enough to help her.

It wasn't that she was afraid the girl would now turn on them but because while Sam only seemed to have eyes for the body, Jessa's attention had stayed on the open window. She had seen the one who had done the throwing, first seemingly admiring what she had done and then noticing Jessa and Sam.

They had locked eyes briefly and even from a distance Jessa felt that primitive part of her brain that reacted the same to just *pictures* of snakes and spiders as it did the real thing, now screaming at her to run. Jessa watched the crazy first disappear from the window and then suddenly launched herself out as well.

Because she had done it deliberately, this woman managed to put a little more strength into her leap, landing past her original victim and slamming into the ground only about a metre away from them.

All of this had taken less than a few seconds and then they were running through the backyard, over the fence to Sam's jeep.

Jessa had sat mutely in the passenger side, just watching the unfolding mayhem around them. She had thought it had been bad on her way back to the share-house but it was a whole new story now as more people were starting to wake up and venture out into the day.

"We need to get out of the city," Sam said again, just as much to himself as to Jessa.

"I want to go home." Jessa's voice sounded small and almost childlike.

"Where do you live?"

Jessa told him and he shook his head. "That's too far away. And even if I wanted to, I don't have enough petrol to cover that distance. I usually only have enough money to keep the gauge a few millimetres off empty anyway. We'll make it to my family though."

"Are they going to be okay...?"

Chapter Nine –

1

"Your parents live here?" Jessa asked, getting out of the car. The kid immediately started to kick his legs out, making it very clear that he now wanted down and Jessa obliged.

"This way," Sam said.

"Are you sure about this?"

"It'll be fine."

"What are all these people doing here?"

"My mother is the mayor. It's possible everyone came here because they didn't know where else to go."

"A bit like us," Jessa muttered. She picked the kid back up and he immediately began protesting loudly. "Hey, stop that," she said. "I know you want to play in the dirt but the adults need to get together and talk about a few..." Jessa had been about to say "things" but as she stared at the woman now jogging their way, she found it difficult to swallow.

There was nothing at all that identified her as Sam's mother but Jessa felt safe in assuming that was correct given the look of extreme relief on Sam's face and the way she pulled him into a strong hug.

She had shoulder-length grey-blonde hair that managed to look both distinguished and care-free – as though she was the kind of person who didn't care about the grey in her hair because she was too cool and too busy to bother. She looked like a person who would be trustworthy enough to be in charge – right down to the high-vis orange vest and rifle she was carrying.

"Oh honey I'm so glad to see you!"

"Mum – what's going on?!"

"We're not sure but we think it might be what your father always talked about."

"Mum, Dad was crazy – "

"Crazy as a fox as it turned out."

Jessa only did a quick glance at the man now joining them, but then did a major double-take when she saw all the weapons he was hauling towards a truck already crammed full of items. He was older than Sam and ladled down with enough artillery to defend a small country it seemed.

"End of the world cultists?" Jessa muttered under her breath before she could stop herself.

Sam glanced at her, causing the other two to eye her up and down.

"Who's she?" the man asked.

"A friend," Sam said.

"We're not taking in strays," he said defiantly, as if it was his final say on the matter. "You should know better Sam."

"*Firstly*, I'm not just 'some stray' he picked up on the side of the road. I'm one of his house-mates from the city. Secondly, even *if* I was some random, why the hell shouldn't he have helped me?!"

"Why the hell should we help you? Why waste resources on a bunch of idiot, namby-pamby cry-babies who have finally come to realize they can't just keep going about their everyday lives thinking and believing someone else is always going to come and take care of 'em?" He got up in her face, forcing Jessa to take a step back even as Sam moved between them.

"Aiden stop!"

"Whether you like it or not little girl it has become survival of the fittest. You need to wake up to that! The world is going to hell in a hand-basket and if you think *anyone* is going to be looking out for anyone else you've got one heavy dose of reality coming!"

Either it was his shouting – or maybe his proximity – but the kid started looking at him first in wonder and then his little face crumbled and he wrapped one of his pudgy arms around her neck, grizzling into her shoulder.

He let out one particularly good wail that even got Aiden glancing in his direction and asking, "What the hell is his problem?"

And that was when Jessa let fly with her own punch, surprising everyone by dropping the older man to the ground.

2

"I've never actually hit anyone before," Jessa said, not sure if she was explaining that she wasn't this type of person or to justify her own surprise.

"Don't worry about it," Sam said with a grin. "He had it coming."

"Who *is* that guy?" She added quickly, " – to *you*, I mean."

Sam's grin got a little wider. "Older brother. I was a bit of a 'turn-of-life-surprise baby – or so my mother puts it. He was grown up and long gone before I showed up, so we don't always get along." He glanced over his shoulder to make sure there was no one close enough to over-hear. "Aiden's always had funny ideas. Our father died when I was four so I don't really remember him that much but from what relatives have told me about the guy, he was more than on his way to having a few screws loose. Aiden naturally spent more time with him so he seems to have gone the same way."

"What about your mother? I mean she must have married the guy for a reason. Is she – ?"

"He wasn't always like that," a voice from behind them said and Jessa wondered if her face came even close to being as red as Sam's when they realized it was his mother.

"I'm Kathleen by the way." She held her hand out

"Jessa."

"Hello Jessa," she said. "I'm afraid we didn't give a very good first impression when you arrived."

"I don't normally hit people either. And I know I shouldn't give excuses for my behaviour but…it's all just been a little stressful."

"Don't be so quick to apologize," Sam said. "It was brilliant to see Aiden get taken down by a girl!"

Kathleen gave him a disapproving look. "Don't gloat to him over that. He's going to be very hard to calm down when he comes to."

"He still hasn't?" Jessa said in surprise.

"You better believe it," Sam said to her. "That's one hell of a right hook you've got!"

Jessa couldn't help but smile back.

"Is the child yours?" Kathleen asked.

"Huh? No. He's just another stray," Jessa joked, not sure if she was on Kathleen's hit list or if she was just as impressed as Sam.

"Where's his mother?'

"I don't know."

"And his father?"

"Dead likely." Jessa worked hard at not recalling the scene in the hospital and was grateful when she managed to reduce the experience to just a few flashes of memory.

"So what is your plan?"

"I don't...know. It's been a busy couple of hours."

Kathleen's face softened. "How did you end up caring for the child?" she asked gently.

Jessa gave her the abridged version and after finishing up said, "And so if you can tell me what to do, that'd be great."

Kathleen fell silent for a few moments and then said slowly, "The child is not yours."

"No – but I feel responsible for him and I'm sure as hell not just going to leave him by the side of the road!"

"And no one is suggesting that," Kathleen said. "I am merely stating the facts. The child is not yours. So technically what you are doing can possibly be construed as kidnapping. You don't even know his name!"

Jessa pressed her lips together tightly.

"However that doesn't matter. It is entirely possible the mother is looking for her child, however it is just as possible that she is dead already or like one of those cannibal ones, eating people – "

"What?!" Sam looked alarm and stared at his mother with shock.

"That's what the news said. So the question becomes, what are you going to do with him?"

Jessa felt uncomfortable. "What do you want me to say? I feel responsible for him – I know that's probably taking it too far on my original offer to help out the guy – and I certainly don't want to adopt the kid. I just...I don't know. I've haven't planned any of this out. Truthfully I just want to get home to my mother. She'll know what to do...who to call...or whatever."

"Is she part of the government?" Sam asked.

"No."

"So what makes you think she'll know what to do?"

Jessa shrugged. "She's a mother. Aren't they supposed to know everything?"

Kathleen smirked, although it didn't last long as she observed the actions of those around them.

Several more people had arrived since her altercation with Sam's brother, mostly ignoring Jessa's interloping and going about their business quickly and efficiently and like this situation wasn't something they were shocked by.

"You guys *are* doomsday preppers, aren't you?" she asked Sam.

"Kind of."

"But you always used to make fun of that show whenever we watched it."

Sam's face flushed slightly and opened his mouth but was interrupted by yelling.

"Get out of my way – I'm going to snap her damn neck!"

Aiden came storming out of nowhere, his eyes blazing and dirt on his face from when he had hit the ground only making them even more noticeable. Jessa cringed, knowing she wasn't going to get a second chance of catching him off-guard and not sure if there was anyone else here going to come to her defence.

Sam however, had his hands balling into fists and looked willing – until Kathleen moved between them and took control as only a mother could have.

"You will do no such thing Aiden Lucas Rutherford," she said, somehow stopping the bigger man in his tracks. "While I don't condone what she did to you, I must applaud her ability to get the better of you. You have been trained – or so you told me when I asked if you were paying attention during drills – and yet she was able to easily sucker punch you with virtually no experience whatsoever!" She glanced over her shoulder at Jessa to confirm this and Jessa nodded.

"That's what I assumed," she said, turning back to Aiden. Her voice wasn't shouting exactly, but she did seem to be getting louder and thus, her voice carrying to everyone else in the nearby vicinity, some of whom were pretending they weren't watching and those who were staring with their mouths wide open.

"If you were even half as good as you thought then maybe I wouldn't have to spend quite as much time worrying about whether or not you are doing something reckless!" Her tone was no longer angry and if anything, she sounded close to tears and Aiden's face flushed and he looked ashamed. "Now, don't you have other things you should be doing?"

"Mum, I – "

"No Aiden, I don't want to hear it. Just go." Kathleen turned back to Jessa. "You also need to make some difficult choices I'm afraid my dear."

Jessa frowned.

"A lot of people are dying or dead," Kathleen tried again.

"You don't have to tell me – I've already seen – "

"And in all likelihood that also includes your mother."

Jessa closed her mouth with a snap and could practically feel her stubbornness close around her like a shield through which no logic could penetrate.

"In which case trying to get to her is likely to be nothing more than a fool's errand." Kathleen looked at her gently but all Jessa wanted to do was slap her. "And it's not just yourself you have to worry about anymore. Where is your mother anyway – where does she live?"

Jessa only glared at her.

"Okay, you don't have to tell me but I'm guessing the fact you came here first meant we're closer – and we are out in the middle of nowhere. Which means you're intending to embark on a fairly strenuous trip, facing who knows what, with a small child in tow."

"What are you getting at?"

"I am trying to make you see that you will never make it."

"Mother!" Sam looked shocked.

"No Sam. Like it or not, in the matter of a few hours the world has become significantly harsher and as a result we are also going to have to be a little harsher."

"What do you want from me?" Jessa asked.

"I don't *want* anything from you. What I'm *offering* is a chance to come with us."

3

"It's a cabin out on the edge of nothing," Sam explained.

"Everyone here is going to try and fit into one little cabin?" Jessa asked blandly. Truthfully her mind was a whirl. A part of her wanted to stay strong and be loyal to her mother but it was also accurate that the only reason she had survived this long was due to luck.

"Not exactly," Sam said. "There's are also two smaller ones and everyone else will be using tents and campervans. The whole point is to be as mobile as possible, ready to bug out at a moment's notice."

"Please don't take this the wrong way and I apologize in advance but I can think of no other way to word this. Was your father, a little...insane?"

"He certainly a few Bradys short of a bunch, or only had one oar in the harbour." He gave Jessa a nudge. "Or however the saying goes. But I guess I can't make fun of him anymore. He got some of it right, didn't he?"

"...do you think I'm a fool?" she asked. "For wanting to go home, I mean."

"...yes," Sam said finally. "But it's all well and good for me to say this when I'm surrounded by my own family. Hell, the first and only thing *I* thought of when the shit hit the fan was getting here and I don't think anything could have stood in my way!" He touched her arm gently. "But that still doesn't mean I want you to go. Jessa seriously...you really need to think about this because like Mum said, in all likelihood – "

"She's already dead. I heard the first time. But like *you* said: if it was *your* family...*your* mother..." Her eyes trailed back to watch the kid playing in the dirt, running his hand through the dust and letting it pour thought his hands fingers again and again. To Jessa it just looked like he was getting himself all dusty, but guessed she should have just been happy he wasn't eating it.

"What about him?" Sam asked after following her eye-line. "We really would look after the kid and he would be safe with us. And you would probably have a much easier time making it without him weighing you down..."

4

Jessa adjusted the straps on the backpack but there was really no chance of her making the extreme weight comfortable. Once Sam and his family had learnt of her decision to go out on her own, she had to admit they had rallied around her, donating things and helping without comment – or complaint. Okay, Aiden had protested a little but even from him it seemed only token and like the sole reason he was against this was because he didn't like her.

They had packed her a *proper* backpack, filling it with supplies she would need. Jessa meanwhile had been watching the kid who had reached the edge of sleepiness and fighting against it every time his eyelids drooped down. It was adorable and was making Jessa feel even more confused about her choices.

'I never promised to look after him for the rest of my life! And I sure as hell can't take him with me. Sam is right – there are plenty of mothers and grandmothers her to look after him. And what if something happens to me?! What if the kid ends up all alone – or picked up by the kind of person who *isn't* good and sells him on a corner to the highest bidder?!'

"Are you sure you don't mind taking him?" she asked Kathleen who was busy with her body half in the backseat, half out as she struggled to fit even more things into an overly-packed car – apparently she hadn't quite adhered to the memo from Sam's father about travelling light.

"Not a problem," Kathleen responded, slightly muffled but still audible. "I'm sure some of the older ladies would really like having someone to look after."

Jessa very much wanted to believe this but these were all strangers to her.

'So's the kid.' Jessa shook her head, angry that no matter how many times she went over this, it just seemed to be a circular argument.

"Okay kid," she said, deciding to get this over and done with. "You're going somewhere safe where you will be able to camp for a couple of weeks – maybe even *years* considering what everyone is saying. That'll be fun, won't it? You'll get to play in the dirt and breathe fresh air and…and not have to worry about TV or getting likes on snapchat or any of that other crap that seemed so important only a couple of hours ago."

The kid was focussed on making lines or some other kind of pattern that only made sense to him in the dirt. But there must have been a change in her voice because he glanced up at her, staring with wide eyes.

"I know you don't know any of these people, but you didn't know me yesterday – and look how that worked out! I have to trust these people to do right by you and make sure nothing bad happens, okay?"

He gurgled with all four of his teeth, drool coming out and adding to his already stained shirt. Jessa found herself on the verge of tears and couldn't have said why. So before she could succumb to them, she held her arms out to the kid who willingly toddled towards her, throwing his pudgy little arms wide. Jessa hugged him for a few moments, telling herself this was for the best.

"You don't have to leave him," Sam said quietly from behind her. "You can come with us."

"We've been through this," Jessa said, grateful her voice sounded normal. She stood up with the kid in her arms. "They *will* look after him though, right Sam? *You* will?"

"I know you want me to promise that everything is going to be okay and that nothing is going to happen to the little guy but it would be like me trying to get a promise from you that you're going to be fine and stay alive and somehow find us again when you've got your mother. It doesn't work that way anymore – if it *ever* did." He bent down slightly so he could catch her eye and make sure she was looking at him. "I can promise you that I'll do my best though."

"Okay," Jessa said. She bounced the baby a couple of times on her hip and then leant toward Sam so she could hand over the kid.

He went willingly like always and Sam automatically made faces at him.

'Cute,' Jessa thought and then with a small wave to Sam as he kept the kid distracted, walked away.

She had thought it would be hard to keep her back turned and not want to have one last look over her shoulder.

'I *don't* love the kid,' she reminded herself. 'So it doesn't matter. I don't have to worry about him anymore. That he might hurt himself – or that someone else might come along and hurt him. I can walk all through the night in the pouring rain and eat only potato chips and soft drink if I want. Maybe I can look for a car and then –

And that was when she heard a sudden, loud scream from behind her.

5

It wasn't a scream of a pain or really even fear – although she supposed that was part of it. Even though she had only spent little more than twenty-four hours with the kid, Jessa was pretty sure she knew what his problem was this time and so didn't immediately turn around like she would have if she had suspected he was under attack.

Instead she told herself to treat this like she was a mother leaving her kid for their first day at school – sure, they might have been screaming and crying now but after a few minutes they would get distracted and move on.

'After all, I am *not* the kid's mother – why the hell should he give a damn about me?!'

Jessa moved faster thinking all she needed to do was get out of his eye-line and then he would give-up and one of the mothers would figure out a way to soothe him and it would all be fine. The piercing shrieks only became louder though – so much so that Jessa actually cringed as she broke into a run on the steep, gravelled road and almost fell over in her haste to get out of there.

She ducked behind a tree that was wide enough to hide her body, catching her breath in the vain hope that after a few minutes she would hear the child's cries subside. If anything though, they only seemed to get louder and Jessa slumped down to a crouch so she could put her hands over her ears.

'People are going to hear this,' she realized – and she didn't just mean neighbours. She and Sam had not seen any of the crazies since they had left the city – in fact once they had left the main road they hadn't seen any other people in general until they had pulled up here. But that didn't mean they weren't still out there. Circling them right now and –

'And if that is the case than the best thing to do is get as far away from the kid and all the noise as fast as possible,' Jessa told herself. 'If there *are* crazies around, than he's going to draw them straight here! And Aiden isn't going to like that! He might find a way to shut the kid up. A permanent solution. Then – '

And Jessa suddenly found herself up and running back towards the cars.

6

The kid didn't quite stop screaming upon seeing her but he did decrease enough to fall under the heading of wailing rather than out and out screeching, especially once she took him back. Kathleen had tried to wave her off, telling her to keep going but Jessa had taken one look at the kid's tear-stained, red and straining face and the way he had lunged for her as soon as she was close, causing Sam to have to scramble to make sure he didn't drop him.

Which was why she found herself standing on the driveway of their now vacated house, watching as the small group slowly departed one by one. Sam made sure they were the last to leave and while Aiden who was behind the wheel completely ignoring her, Sam continued to yell advice out the window. Oddly Kathleen was refusing to even look at her and Jessa wondered if she was taking the rejection personally and had liked the kid.

"Not that *I* like you," she said to him. "I have no idea why I came back, just so you know. My life would be so much easier if you weren't around. And you would have been far better off with them too." Her voice had a strange crack to it like she was on the verge of bursting into tears. "They know what they were doing and they especially weren't heading off to do something as suicidal as I am."

Suddenly it all became too much and she gave up trying to hold in the sob that had been threatening all along. She clung to the kid, rubbing his back in a way that was supposed to be soothing to him but really, it was comforting her.

"Damn, kid," she muttered into his shirt before giving herself a mental slap. "Get it together Jess!"

When she pulled back the kid was looking at her with his bottom lip out and quivering slightly. Then he put his hand on her face, looking solemn.

"You know I'm just going to get us killed, right?" she said, not sure why she was so sure it was true. "Or maybe you'll just get me killed. Either way kid, you seriously picked the losing side."

Chapter Ten –

1

Jessa realized she still had no transport and *now* really needed some. While it wasn't exactly late in the day – hell, it wasn't even late in the morning! – Jessa felt like it would be a good idea to find somewhere to rest. Maybe have a little snooze, rather than trying to keep going and since she now knew for a fact the next-door neighbour's house was empty – they had been among the group with Sam's family – she went there.

Unfortunately Jessa hadn't spent her formative years breaking into houses or learning such skills she realized were probably going to be of great use now. She assumed it couldn't be *that* difficult considering some of the less than intelligent people at her school who she knew who got their jollies that way and she didn't even have to be stealthy considering the place was deserted. All she needed to do was break a window! However she hadn't anticipated just how clingy the kid would now be, screaming the minute she went to put him down.

So she had to try to break the glass one-handed *and* shield the kid *and* then not drop him when the sharp crash made them both jump. Then Jessa discovered *true* difficulty, trying to climb through the small space balancing not just herself, but the kid and barely managed to keep from landing in the collection of broken glass now carpeting the floor.

The previous family had cleaned out a lot of things but surprisingly left behind the more basic staples. There was bread, ham and milk in the fridge, some cheese and lettuce and after digging far in the back, Jessa was even able to come up with a bottle of beer.

"Can't complain about it not being my brand," she said to the kid. "I haven't drunk enough beer to pick one…and now I probably never will if the world really has gone bust, right?"

Trying to make sandwiches while balancing the kid *had* proved to be beyond her, but she discovered that if she put him on the bench and stayed close by, he was okay.

"Just don't wriggle off, yeah?" she advised him. "You're going to have to be a little more careful with yourself now that you've decided to throw in with me. I barely have any first aid training and I sure as hell won't know how to set an arm if you opt to take a tumble."

The kid was too busy with his hand almost wrist deep in a jar of chocolate spread to care what she was saying though – while still glancing up periodically to check she was within reach Jessa noted with amusement.

"This might be our last decent meal for a while too, so you might want to make it last." Keeping that in mind for herself Jessa wondered if she should continue to use up all the food in the house and make as many sandwiches as possible, or would that just mean carrying around a bunch of rotten food?

"I'm certainly learning how to make important decisions, aren't I?" she said. She picked the kid up, surprisingly not giving a damn about the chocolate spread and how he was going to get it all over her clothes.

They went into a living room where the only evidence that the occupants left in a hurry was some high heels that had been flung into the corner and some odd marks on the wall that showed where decorations had only recently been removed.

'Maybe fancy guns,' Jessa thought but otherwise only had eyes for the oversized couch that almost could have doubled as a single bed.

"They must have been a family of line-backers to need a couch that big, don't ya think?" she asked the kid. When she sat down on it and moved far enough to rest against the back, her feet no longer touched the floor and it would have been difficult for her to climb out even if she *hadn't* had been so fatigued.

"I should go do something about that window," she mumbled to herself. But her eyes were already starting to droop.

"I need to secure the kid too." Her eyes were already half closed. "He might just go wandering around by himself." They were completely closed now. "He could hurt himself." Her chin fell to rest on her chest. "Or someone could come in through the window and..."

And she was gone.

2

"You really are something special kid, you know that?" Jessa had woke up from a dead sleep, her heart pounding in her chest from a nightmare that had slipped away like sand through her fingers the minute she had sat up. Not that she minded. She had enough fears of her own without being chased by imaginary ones once she realized it was dark. And she was alone.

She had found the kid it one of the ground floor bedrooms, a little girl stuck in the 'in-between' stage of soft toys and the potentially slightly more grown up world of my-little-ponies by the looks of it. He had been pacing around the edges of the bed set only about a foot off the floor and with a top blanket of pink fluffy clouds and a princess castle.

She had no idea what he had done all day – possibly had a nap himself, or spent the day making broom-broom noises while pushing a princess carriage around on the floor, minus the horse which he demonstrated to her several times.

Either way he was cheerful and after cautiously checking the house was still empty, Jessa reassessed her situation. Considering she had slept almost the entire day away it would have been ridiculous to head out in the middle of the night so she had settled in.

The first thing was to properly barricade the window by wrestling a small end-table against the hole made and tying it there with curtains. It wasn't totally secure now but at least it was going to take a little more effort for someone to break in. From there she had gone around closing all the curtains in the place and then lighting a fire in the living room.

"This is a time of 'firsts', isn't it kid," she said. "I'm sure you will be pleased to know that this is the first time I have ever had to light a fire! Okay, I did it in a fireplace and with matches but it still counts! And it's not bad for a chick who had never had anything to do with girl-scouts or anything!"

The kid was watching the fire-light, absolutely fascinated. Jessa feared this was going to translate into him going over to try and touch it when she wasn't looking but her grandmother's voice was there in her head, metaphorically rolling her eyes.

'What if he does?' Gran asked. 'He'll only do it once and then the lesson will be learnt.'

Jessa half laughed, half rolled her eyes too.

"Just be careful, okay kid?...You know what? I think it's about time we figure out a name for you...any preferences? I don't think we should go with anything too old-fashioned – you are a young man on the up and up after all. It should still be classic though and not pretentious like those posers who name their kids things like Atticus or Sawyer. Unfortunately of course I can't do the thing of giving you a family name from *your* line and I've never really liked any of the names that run in *my* family...we could always go simple...John? Whadda ya think little guy?"

She pulled him into her lap. "It'd be easy and quick to yell if I see you getting into trouble. And I should be able to remember it...you don't really *look* like a John though."

The kid in question put a pudgy fist into his mouth and started sucking on it. Jessa was fairly certain this meant he was getting tired and ready for a nap.

"What about Cade?! It's unusual and different – but not entering the realm of rock stars who name their kids after cities or food-groups. It's short and I think indicates a kind of toughness and strength which might be just what you need in this new world. In case you're wondering it was going to be the name of one of my little cousins if she turned out to be a boy. But she was a girl and so the poor thing got called Priscilla – I know right, what the hell is that?! But Cade is nice and cool and I think should serve you well. What – no objections?" The kid was asleep. "Okay, Cade it is," she said. "At least it's better than my second choice: Billy...Billy the Kid...get it?"

Chapter Eleven –

1

"Cade I'm telling you right now, this would be so much easier if you were a little bit younger or older. As it is, at this age, you kind of suck."

At least his youth meant she could say things like this to him and not have to worry about hurting his feelings. But that didn't do much to placate the ache in her shoulders from having to carry the kid in a sling across her chest even though he truly was too big and he tended to wriggle around, wanting to get out and see the world or just walk for himself.

She was already overloaded like a pack-horse with the food she had taken from the house, spare clothes and a tent Sam had insisted she take even though she wasn't sure she would be able to put one up. She still carried it though, afraid she would run into Sam and he would immediately ask where it was.

She was also carrying two knives tucked into her belt, one more wrapped in a tea towel in her backpack and another much smaller one tucked into her boot. She didn't know whether to be irritated or grateful Sam's neighbours hadn't left behind a gun for her to 'borrow' too. On the one hand it would have been nice to have a decent weapon but she had never been a big fan of guns, being of the frame of mind that they only escalated already bad situations – especially if they fell into the wrong hands.

"And I don't know anything about them," she admitted to Cade. "So it's probably for the best since no doubt I would end up shooting my hand off!"

Something else that no doubt would have made her life a lot easier would have been putting Cade in a pram to push him around. Unfortunately several problems revealed themselves with that one, including the simple detail that she hadn't been able to find one. Even the sling she was using now was technically a bedsheet she had folded into a triangle to achieve the desired effect. Him walking was out of the question considering he moved about a metre every ten minutes.

"And I kind of want to reach home before next year, okay?" Cade gurgled happily once she gave him a toy she had swiped from the house, a play-phone that made noises when the numbers were pressed. "If nothing else I guess I'm going to be in terrific shape by the end of all this."

It had of course occurred to her to get a car but unlike her original escape from the hospital, there weren't many just lying around with the keys in the ignition. Jessa was actually surprised by this because in most apocalypse movies it seemed like there were abandoned cars left, right and centre. All "survivors" had to do was grab one – and then worry about the aliens or the vampires or whatever the hell else they were running from in order to qualify it as an Armageddon tale.

Jessa had ran into a few of what she was deeming The Crazies but she had ducked behind things until they found something else that interested them – their short attention spans really was turning out to be in Jessa's favour.

And then there were the others like her.

She didn't know any of their intended destinations – since there wasn't really any way to tell a normal person from a crazy one until getting up close and Jessa had adopted the strategy of assuming the worst and avoiding all. And she wasn't the only one to come to this conclusion with several incidents of her rounding a corner seeing someone up ahead, them spotting her and suddenly turning tail and running. Jessa actually found it borderline amusing but also a little depressing as she wondered what was becoming of people.

"If we keep this up I'm not even sure we're going to be able to come back from this," she told Cade. "People need to come together to rebuild society or whatever!"

It was morning but making its way towards midday as Jessa munched on a bag of chips, doing her best not to let crumbs fall into

Cade's hair from her own eating and occasionally giving him one to eat when he waved his pudgy hand. "Okay-okay! But just so you know, you don't want to go and put on any *more* weight or this little carrier service you've got going is going to be over."

"You know, I've been thinking: maybe we can try for a bicycle – I know it still won't be that fast and I'm not entirely sure how well you'll balance in the basket...or maybe I can find one with one of those child seats in the back and – "

The sound of yelling made Jessa's head to snap to the side like it was an automatic chain-reaction. Part of her wanted to run in the opposite direction but another more self-destructive side was thinking about how it had been so long since she had seen another person – and she still didn't understand what was going on and needed more information. And this could potentially be attained by finding out what the yelling was about.

Another voice – definitely male – joined the fray, followed by the sound of breaking glass. "I know I'm only asking for trouble kid but who knows, maybe they can help us. What do you think?"

Naturally he agreed with everything she said. "And that is part of the reason why I like your company so much," she murmured as she figured out the yelling was coming from around the side of a building and moved closer, trying to use it as cover.

2

She ran the length of the wall, Cade bouncing along with her and feeling more than a little absurd.

And then the closer she got, the more sure she became that this was a bad idea.

She had seriously miscalculated the amount of people involved in this particular melee – the group looked to be about thirty or so, not counting the ones in the car that the mob had surrounded or the small groups of children off to the side who were watching the entire scene unfold with shell-shocked looks.

The small family in the car must have been taking what looked like everything that might have been in their house that wasn't nailed down.

"See, they were driving along all nice and pleasant," Jessa said, not really aware she was speaking, much less in a hushed, pleasant voice like she was telling Cade a bedtime story. "Taking the backroads in the hopes that they would avoid crowds of people they had heard on the radio who were starting to become dangerous. Not *necessarily* like the Crazies but just as dangerous in their own way. They're scared and want a car – *their* car specifically. Why don't they have their own? – maybe they all got caught in a traffic jam on the highway."

The mob had surrounded the car, preventing it from being able to go any further and were now pushing on it from either side so it was rocking.

"Anyway they're tired of walking on foot and they want *this* car to get them wherever they want to go." Truthfully Jessa wasn't sure if they were thinking on such finer terms and not were merely reacting to the mob-frenzy of panic and bloodlust taking over. After all, how was it going to serve them to smash the windows of the car they were going to commandeer for themselves? Sure, it now meant they were able to reach the occupants inside and drag out what looked like an eight year old girl through the window despite all the desperate attempts of her older sister to hold onto her, but it also meant that anyone else could do exactly the same thing to *them* once they got in the car!

Jessa wanted to keep focussing on their foolishness so she could pretend she didn't notice the way the small girl was screaming in terror as her arm caught on the glass as she was roughly pulled, gouging it and causing a surprising amount of blood to pour out.

Jessa was half afraid the Dad might now drive off, seizing the chance to escape as the crowd descended on the girl, but the father had not been so willing to forgo his daughter and made the mistake of unlocking the doors and leaving the confines to attempt a rescue.

Maybe they *would* have been better off staying in the car and using it as a weapon since he and his wife only leapt straight into the arms of the waiting horde.

Both Jessa and Cade watched with equally wide eyes as the people attacked the couple much more viciously than they had the little girl, laying into them with fists and kicks and make-shift weapons. If they had used teeth than Jessa would have mistaken them for Crazies but then, after the parents were prone on the ground, one of the younger guys dived into the open car door. The old man who's arm he had ducked under let out a roar and reached for him but the young guy slammed his foot on the accelerator. The car leapt forward, taking out the people directly in front and then a quick reverse shift had taken out the ones behind as well. By now a couple of his buddies had also dived in, one even taking the risk of jumping through the broken window at the back.

Jessa lost track of how many of them made it into the vehicle before the guy in the driver's seat became impatient and just gunned it even though the older teenage sister was still in the back seat, screaming in terror.

"Don't worry kid, they're just gonna drive a little bit up the road and then let her get out," Jessa murmured, not sure why she was bothering to lie. "She'll be back with her family in no time and then they're just going to have to find another way to get where they were going."

Jessa turned away from the view as much for herself as for the kid, not wanting either of them to have to watch as the crowd took out their frustration at having lost the car on its previous occupants. The sounds of their screams followed Jessa as she walked away and she had to repeat to herself over and over again that there was nothing she could do. Nothing at all. Not one thing.

"I already have enough problems," she explained to Cade. "And I'm not a fighter so I can't help those people. I'm *not* Pied-Piper collecting orphans! It's a hard world, just like Kathleen said...it just...is."

3

Jessa tried to make herself feeling better by listing the benefits of walking the entire way home.

"I mean sure, it's going to take for absolute ever but no noise means we won't attract any unwanted attention. A motorbike for the same reason."

Jessa had only ever ridden a motorbike twice in her life and one of those had been when she was nine and clinging to the back of her cousin's shirt while he rode around his backyard. Her mother had yelled blue murder when she had spotted them and while everyone else had laughed at the 'city-people' and all their fears and cautions, truthfully Jessa had been kind of scared herself and hadn't tried it again until several years later when she had been sixteen and one of the guys at school had got themselves a little moped and was giving some of the girls a go.

That time Jessa had felt a little better with the wind in her hair but it had also been without the added worry of a baby in the back seat – supposing she could even *find* one with a back seat. It amused her temporarily to picture finding one with a side-car and securing Cade in *that* but it would also cancel out the mobility of a two-wheeled transportation.

"Nah, it's better if we just stay on foot," Jessa continued. "So long as the weather holds out and all those *properly* crazy people continue to stick to the city, we should be okay. Right kid?...right."

"Besides, the most a bike can carry has to fit in a small basket on the front or that rack thing on the back. We have to leave a great deal of this stuff behind and foraging off the land like we're on 'Survivor' might be well and good but we're not exactly surrounded by fruit trees on every corner! Or have time to stop and fish or pick snails and fry them up

– although I'll say now I'm going to be pretty damn hungry...I'd break into a 7-11 before I would get *that* desperate...although I guess with no police around little things like *laws* no longer apply, do they?" she asked, thinking about the family.

Chapter Twelve –

1

"Honestly never thought I would get so good at this my man," Jessa said as she continued to work the knots. While at first she may have felt guilty about breaking and entering into people's houses, when measured against having to spend the night outside and being able to go to sleep without worrying about waking up to find people either stealing their stuff or trying to kill them – her morals soon quietened down.

She only wished the paranoid voice in her head was so easily placated as no matter how tired she was or what a long day it had been – or how *safe* the house *looked* – it still insisted she go around each time, securing all the doors and windows and setting up ridiculous booby traps that any sane person or a slight measure of common sense would have found laughable. Pieces of string spread out across the room like some kind of laser-maze; chairs tied up against doors; knick-naks on window sills that would create noise if someone tried to sneak in.

"I don't think it will be an issue though," she continued, trying to soothe herself as much as the kid. "We haven't seen too many signs of people at night, have we?"

But they weren't the *only* people left and Jessa had broken down what remained of society into three categories:

1. **The mob people who were infected or sick or maybe just temporarily insane for all she knew –**

These were scary and dangerous and altogether not that smart and with the average attention span of a two year old with ADHD. It was beyond hazardous if they spotted you, but if you managed to outrun them or simply get out of their field of vision, than you were okay. And they definitely weren't big on the whole gang thing as they seemed just as likely to attack and hurt each other as they were regular people.

"So at least it's not a complete US versus THEM mentality," she mentioned to Cade after they had watched three separate incidents of this. "And three proves a pattern," she added. "My old science teacher Mr Turner said so."

1. Scared, normal people.

People who were still largely normal and just doing their best to survive in a world that had undergone a rather sudden and drastic shift. These ones tended to move in very small groups – Jessa thought she had seen one group with as many as four people but she couldn't be sure. Because that was the other thing: people who belonged to this group did their upmost to shun any and all contact with any others.

"It's almost like we move around like scared little mice," was how Jessa described it when she had been in a less than positive frame of mind after an scene involving a small shopping trolley. She had spotted it in someone's front yard and thought it would be good to put Cade and some of their stuff in for a while and push along. Not a permanent solution but maybe enough to give her back a small break after so many hours. Unfortunately someone else had spotted it at the same time – an old woman looking like she'd had a particularly hard time of it over the past few days.

Jessa had been willing to be generous and let the woman have it considering it seemed to be so important to her, screeching like a banshee when she saw Jessa was going to get there first and causing Jessa to assume she was actually one of the crazies. She had raised her 'weapon' automatically – a wrench she had requisitioned after rummaging through garage.

The woman had then instantly dropped to the ground as though Jessa had already hit her, cowering but making sounds Jessa was finally able to recognize as words: "Mine, it's mine!"

"Yeah, sure, whatever," Jessa had said, walking away confused.

And *then* there was the service station incident. The place had been ransacked but interestingly it didn't look like too much had been taken – it was more like someone had just trashed the place, maybe looking for cash or something equally as pointless in this new arrangement and leaving behind what Jessa deemed far more important – food and drink.

She had just been in the middle of trying to convince the kid that he couldn't have a sip of her Energy Drink – she didn't even want to think about how hyped he would get on *that* – when someone had climbed in through the broken window. Jessa had been sitting on the floor with the kid near the refrigerators, frozen like it was a game of Simon Says.

In fact, she had been so still that the first time he saw her, his eyes kept going and it was only during the second sweep that he finally did a double-take. Up until then Jessa had been debating over whether or not she could take him – he looked like a sixty year old hippie-vegan who hadn't had a decent meal in decades. His eyes had flickered briefly to Cade, then back to her and then around the place at all the food and drink. They had both stared as though weighing each other up as she slowly stood up, wishing she had cleared a little of the aisle so if it came down to a fight that she would have had room to move.

Instead though, the guy just carefully backed up and then out of the window again. Jessa was afraid he was going out to get back-up but as she got the courage to peer out the window herself, she saw he was just sitting by his bike – a yellow nostalgia one with a basket with flowers on the front Jessa saw with amusement – his arms crossed over his chest but otherwise appearing harmless and doing absolutely nothing but waiting.

"He's giving us a chance to pick out what *we* want," Jessa murmured in surprise. In fact, he was even being so gentlemanly about it that he was waiting in the rain! It was only a slight downpour but after spending a few days on the road Jessa had come to understand the importance of being dry.

So, taking a chance – and hoping against hope this wasn't just some kind of trick, she waved to get his attention and then motioned him inside.

He had hesitated for almost a full minute before moving at a snail's pace towards her. For every step he took, Jessa took one backwards until before too long they were in exactly the same positions they had started in – Jessa pressed up against the refrigerator wall of drinks, him crouched just inside the window but otherwise motionless.

What had followed had been quite possibly the strangest meal Jessa had ever experienced. They had waited out the rain-shower together, which has lasted approximately forty minutes, neither saying a single word even as hunger got the better of them and they chowed down on chips and sweets, him staying on his side of the room, Jessa and Cade staying on theirs. They had continued to circle each other warily, as though waiting for any kind of sign that the other's mood was about to turn but simultaneously, it was as though each of them had been missing the company of another human being and so it was oddly comforting.

The rain had eventually stopped and the man had left first and when Jessa had stepped outside, there had been a small plastic bag of apples leaning against the same light pole the man had lent his bike against. It hadn't necessarily been a grand gesture, but it had touched her just the same. She called out a thankyou even though all around her appeared to be deserted and despite the brevity of the experience, it was something her mind kept going back to when she needed to hope that people could still be good.

Because then finally there were:

1. **Evil humans**

These were actually the ones who scared her most of all. They were the people who were still normal but had not held onto their humanity. Or maybe they had been evil and horrible people to begin with and the breakdown of society hadn't made much of a difference to them. Jessa could believe that – after all, the only thing someone had to do was watch news headlines to wonder what was happening to the world.

These were the ones responsible for the time she had been walking down a sidewalk, darting from store front to store front feeling ridiculous but at the same time, unable to fight the urge that this was safer. She had heard the sound of the car revving and hidden in the shadows, watching as several of the crazy-ones had been drawn to the deep rumble.

Jessa had been trapped but luckily none of them had come even close to looking her way, instead just making their way to the main road, shuffling in the direction of the noise like lemmings. The car came swerving around the bend, Jessa staring as the driver treated the crazies as though he was playing a game of grand theft auto, mowing them down like they were nothing.

This would have been bad enough on its own except Jessa had a strong feeling the driver wouldn't have cared *who* was falling under the wheels of his car – crazies *or* regular people.

But that one had been *nothing* compared to today. She had been taking the backstreets as much as possible and walking past a old gothic church. Or maybe it had actually been a school yard. 'Hell, it could have been a mental institution for all I know,' Jessa thought, her mind once again returning to the incident despite her desperate attempts to think about something – *any*thing – else.

She had been trailing a really tall wall surrounding the property, the wall itself looking as though it had been there since the middle ages as gothic as the church itself. The stones had been dark grey, soaring far above her head and providing some shade from the sun which was usually nice given the cold temperature but Jessa didn't have baby sunglasses and so worried about Cade's eyes. Jessa had glanced upwards, wanting to see the impressive building that was no doubt located inside – and also slightly interested to find out where the noise was coming from.

It was hard to describe beyond it was either a very soft moan or gnawing that almost sounded like droning bees but wasn't. At first the position of the sun meant she hadn't seen anything beyond the rather hazardous looking spikes positioned on top at regular intervals. But then she had spotted a round that seemed to have the noise emanating from it. And then another one next to that. And then another. And then another.

Feeling more curious than afraid she followed the path of the wall, moving near a corner where the shading changed and growing even more confused when she realized the orbs were moving as well as making noises. Then the smell of blood hit her – a scent that was completely unmistakable and which she had become well acquainted with over the past couple of days. She had swallowed thickly and told herself to walk away now. That she didn't need this new nightmare on top of everything else and that it wouldn't serve her in any way to know for sure what was up there. But her feet had moved independently and before too long, she was standing directly below one of the columns, leaning against the wall slightly.

Heads. Crazy-people heads – or maybe more specifically: zombie heads if she was finally going to admit what was going on and since there could be no other possible explanation as to why the severed heads that had been crudely decapitated from their original owners could still be moving – growling and straining to bite even though they were nothing from the neck down.

There were at least eight more heads running the gamut of the wall before it reached another sharp angle and then continued on. Jessa wasn't sure if there were any heads along that side as well, although envisioned whoever had done this working on creating a whole set along the entire outer perimeter.

'And how do you know they're going to only go after crazies?' a panicked voice from within her asked. 'Hell, maybe it was one of the crazies who did this! It's the kind of thing they do now!'

Jessa was pretty sure it wasn't them though, considering they didn't seem particularly 'creative'. They just killed, ate and then moved on.

Nevertheless a cold sweat broke out on the back of her neck and she had to fight the urge to scream or cry or simply set fire to the whole wall – if not the building itself – just to put the people up there out of their misery.

Instead though she just slowly backed away, managing to keep from bolting until one of the heads let out a particularly loud moan and what had suspiciously sounded like a desperate call for help.

2

"But it wasn't real, I'm sure of it," Jessa was saying to Cade. "They *don't* talk, I know that. All they do is make those strange growling sounds or grunts if they're out of shape...kind of like gorillas. Not that gorillas really act like that – or maybe acted might be a better word considering I'm not sure how many of them might still be around."

"I hope they're still around. Gorillas were kind of cool. In fact a lot of animals were, but maybe being from the same species tree they might be affected by whatever this is too. Actually maybe this was all originally some kind of ape infection that has somehow mutated and crossed over – like that avian flu or that one that started with pigs. For that matter, I hope there are still some pigs – not all of them were nice but the little tiny ones that could fit into tea-cups were pretty cute."

Cade kicked out with his legs to show how much interest he had in this particular topic. In fact, he lashed out so hard he ended up kicking Jessa slightly in the groin.

"Don't do that!...No you can't get down....because when I put you down and you try to do some walking it takes us five minutes to get about two feet...besides, you'll just get tired and plonk yourself down suddenly and I'll have to put you back in the sling anyway. Come on kid, we need to get out of this city before nightfall or be stuck trying to break into an apartment. And those things will be a lot harder to get into!"

Jessa didn't know this for a fact but it seemed likely considering the windows weren't exactly accessible like they were on houses. And then of course, there was her whole issue of being in a city.

She heard a sound behind her – not a big sound but enough to catch her notice in the otherwise quiet surroundings that had previously only contained her footsteps and the occasional gurgle from Cade. In fact, half the reason why she had even been talking to him was to fill the silence with *something*. Now though, she was sure she had heard the scuffle. A foot 'catching' on a raised bit of footpath maybe; or a shoe kicking a piece of rubbish. It had seemed accidental, maybe like someone following her but doing their best to hide it.

Instead of being subtle, Jessa suddenly dived into a shop entrance, hugging her body against the wall and trying to shield Cade as best she could. The door was locked so there she was now trapped, angry at her stupidity of cornering herself.

Jessa heard the scuffling sound again and a sharp intake of breath. Jessa had a split-second decision to stay or try to run and before she'd even processed what she was going to do, she was out and running.

It was as though one minute she had been crouched in the dark, her knees aching from this position and the next she had been running along the pavement, still surprisingly quiet to her ears but already feeling as though this wasn't going to work. While all the extra walking might have made her fitter and stronger, there was just no way she was going to be able to outrun someone else – least of all with the kid.

She thought she heard someone gaining distance behind her but didn't dare to look over her shoulder to check, instead holding Cade closer to her body. A sinister suggestion flittered through her mind that she would probably run a lot faster if she just dropped Cade – but she held him even tighter to her body to contract this urge, horrified at the thought.

Instead, in an effort to distract herself and keep such nasty impulses away, she started her own chant in her head of 'Don't fall over, don't fall over, don't fall over' in time with her running tempo.

Jessa thought she heard a female voice call out "Hey – no wait!" and then she rounded a corner and faced a scene of utter carnage and chaos.

Chapter Thirteen –

1

Jessa had not seen so many people in one spot since the mob scene and had started to believe there might not be enough normal around. But the two opposed groups of normal and crazies seemed evenly matched. They faced off with each other, the Crazies forming an unintentional pack for once, to confront their enemy.

The dramatic difference in clothing made it easy to distinguish between the two groups. The normal were dressed like her – clothing more for function than style, with backpacks, camping gear and bikes.

The crazies were wearing whatever the hell it was they had been dressed in at the time when things had gone to hell. Clothes that were dirty and bloodied and ripped in several places, injuries that potentially should have – or maybe even did – kill them. They were also the ones now making urgent grunting, growling sounds, chasing down those screaming and trying to get away, riding the backs of others, and seemingly only enjoying themselves when they had their hands buried deep in the chest of a normal person, scooping out their insides. It was almost like kids at a party attacking a piñata and enjoying the gooey prize inside.

Jessa skidded to a stop, falling down like she had been trying to avoid all along and now grateful she was wearing thick jeans, saving her from losing the top layer of skin on her legs.

She was barely two metres away from a trio consisting of two men and a woman, one of them a Crazy as evidenced by the fast-food restaurant uniform he was wearing and the fact he didn't have any shoes and his feet looked cut up and infected.

He was riding the man of the couple, trying to get at his neck with the man holding him off by using one of his hands on the Crazie's throat and locking his arm. This was managing to keep the guy from gnawing off the other's nose but the Crazy still had his hand free to hit at his intended victim and each time he did, it caused the normal man's concentration and strength to slip.

Meanwhile, the female of the couple was being fairly useless, one hand on her mouth screaming, while the other batted at the Crazy with a stick of some kind.

'Seriously?' Jessa thought. The Crazy would not be distracted from his target though. Maybe it was the fresh blood or just the overall carnage of the situation but he was even more worked up than usual.

Jessa tried to kick back on her heels to crab-crawl backwards – she didn't know who or what was behind her but anything had to be better than trying to enter this melee.

'No one to blame but themselves,' she thought, knowing she was being ruthless but at the same time, this was the way it was now. 'If they were stupid enough to walk into this mess then they deserve what they get!'

The woman continued to scream pointlessly as the guy she had been with slowly but surely, lost his fight.

'I don't want to see this.' But Jessa couldn't turn away as the man's arm suddenly gave out, the Crazy biting at him with snapping teeth, eating him from the face down. The man's screams became infinitely more high-pitched as at the same time, the Crazy's own garbled nonsense took on a pleasurable tone.

'Satisfaction,' Jessa thought, unsure of whether it was the kill it was enjoying or the being sated. She felt her stomach clench tight, as though her body was reacting to this scene by pulling in on itself. She half expected that when she tried to move again she would find herself contorted and twisted like a pretzel, unable to unravel.

But instead she leapt up as though she had springs under her body, grabbing the screaming woman by her upper arms and shaking her.

"Stop it! You need to shut up! You need to be quiet – do you hear me?!"

The woman continued to scream unintelligibly though until Jessa considered slapping her across the face.

And then a hand dropped down on *Jessa's* arm.

2

Forgetting all about the importance of keeping quiet – Jessa screamed, assuming the worst and that the Crazy had finished with his original meal and wanted something a little 'fresher'. In fact, she was so sure of this that she actually *felt* the weight of him jumping on her back, trying to drag her down to the ground and hunched over further automatically to compensate.

There was nothing there though and as Jessa looked at the owner of the hand, she was looking into the face of an older woman. She was younger than Jessa's mother, and staring with wide eyes.

"You need to come with me," she said, tugging on her arm and pulling Jessa away from the fighting crowd.

"Come on!" the woman insisted. "NOW!"

Chapter Fourteen –

1

Jessa didn't know why she went with the woman. Maybe it was her resemblance to Jessa's own mother. Or maybe it was far more self-indulgent – Jessa was simply sick and tired of having to make all the life and death decisions and was more than willing to give up the responsibility and let someone else have a go for a while.

It was reckless but at the same time, a blessed – albeit temporary – relief.

The moment she had realized Jessa was going to follow her, the woman had let go and started jogging back the way they had come – although she still kept periodically checking over her shoulder to make sure Jessa was still there. At first Jessa thought she might have been checking to see if they were being followed by some of the Crazies but was then oddly touched when she realized this wasn't the case.

'She's checking to make sure I'm still back here...because she cares and wants to make sure I'm okay.' Jessa felt warm at this and when the woman ducked into a small nook that was pitch black from Jessa's point of view, she followed without any hesitation.

The space was barely wide enough for them to fit shoulder to shoulder and then two steps in, lead up a rather steep staircase. Jessa instantly felt claustrophobic and started to back up a step but her wrist was grabbed again, practically yanking her forward.

"We have to hurry!" the woman said.

'She's going to make sure I don't fall,' Jessa thought and again felt that small sense of comfort. Of course she still would have preferred to be holding the woman's hand nicely rather than the vice-like grip on her wrist. Maybe that way she would have had a little more control over how fast they were going and not lost her footing twice, barely managing to avoid slamming her chin or front teeth into the concrete steps the first time and not able to save her cheek at all on the second.

After three flights of stairs the woman motioned Jessa to the right. The front door was slightly ajar making Jessa nervous about who (or what) could have made its way inside while the woman was out. "Is there anyone else inside?" Jessa asked, keeping her voice low.

"No," she said, moving past Jessa. "Everyone else in the building has either gone or never came back in the first place. You'll be okay here," she said, turning on a miniature flashlight so she could lock the door. She turned the light off again before Jessa had a chance to ask for one of her own and she listened to shuffling of her moving around before a camping lamp was lit.

"Are you sure you should be doing that?" Jessa said anxiously. "What if they see?"

"It's a very dull glow," the woman said and then pointed towards the windows. "And I've put up black-out curtains. After several days of watching them I think they're only attracted to movement. Never once have they entered a house and come looking for people – they just wander up and down the streets most of the time."

"So you've seen a lot of them?"

"A fair few. Not as many as there should be considering the population of the city – although I think there's starting to be more and more each day. I mean, I can't tell for sure – it might just be that I'm counting the same people over and over again."

"Do you think they're making more people crazy, like them?" Jessa was surprised by just how good it felt to finally have someone else to talk this over with.

"No," the woman said. "I mean I don't think it works that way – at least that's not what they were saying on the news. I think there's just more and more of them filtering out of the big city, looking for...something."

"The News?! You mean there's still someone broadcasting?!"

The woman looked a little embarrassed. "No, I meant the radio. And truthfully I'm not sure how much to trust them – they could just be broadcasting their opinion. But they sound official, and they begin each broadcast with a reminder that people should stay in their houses, stockpile supplies and try to wait it out. Martial Law was announced three days ago and before that, a state of National Emergency."

"So everywhere has been affected?"

The woman nodded. "Or *in*-fected anyway."

"Do they know what it is?" Jessa asked.

"Not really." The woman kept glancing down at Cade. "There's been some talk about dead people getting back up again but that's ridiculous. These people have just been infected with something that is making them become violent and brutal."

Jessa thought about the heads on the spikes but kept that to herself. "Are we safe here?" she asked.

"If you mean in my apartment I guess you're as safe here as anywhere else. Like I said before, they're not interested in coming into the building thus far – beyond ripping off the original door – there did used to be a door out the front, people couldn't just walk in off the street. Anyway, a couple of them went running up and down the halls for a few hours but I had the impression they were less looking for people to hurt and more just trying to find a way out. Kind of like they were a trapped bug that had somehow got stuck. Eventually they did...but if you mean safe with me than hopefully you've figured out I'm okay. I saw from up here that you were about to walk into danger and that you had a kid with you – and I wanted to make sure you were okay...how *is* the kid?"

"Fine," she said absently.

"When I saw where you were headed I was going to call out but I was worried you might scream or run."

"You must have been watching me for a while," Jessa said, going to the window herself and very slowly drawing back the curtain to see what was happening on street level. She turned her back on the woman and didn't think anything of it until a hand suddenly grabbed hers and jerked her away from the window so hard and fast she fell back against the wall.

"Careful! – you don't want any of them to see us!"

Jessa stared at her from only inches away, their noses not quite touching but close. "I'm Jessa," she said, trying to figure out if all the danger was out on the street. "I don't think I've introduced Cade..."

It was an odd sense of relief when the woman switched her gaze from Jessa down to the kid and Jessa no longer had to stare directly into her eyes.

"Sheryl."

She had to be in her forties or fifties and was wearing a T-shirt with a christmas elf on it. Jessa tried to overlook this – she wasn't the fashion police after all – and at least she seemed like she had been keeping good personal hygiene which was more than could be said for Jessa who hadn't been able to have a proper shower in over a week. However it was still unnerving how the woman would occasionally look at something else – Jessa, the window, furniture – but her attention always seemed to come back to Cade.

"Um...thank-you for this," Jessa said. "You didn't have to go out of your way to help us so I want you to know that I'm really grateful. We'll be out of your hair by morning – "

"You don't have to go!"

"Well, um...see, we were on our way somewhere – I need to get to my...family and make sure they're okay...um..." Jessa faltered once Sheryl's focus was no longer so avidly on Cade and instead on her face, seemingly not even blinking.

"Are you hungry?" she asked.

"...more tired than anything else...I guess," Jessa said.

"How long have you been travelling?" Sheryl asked, heading for the kitchen anyway.

"I'm not entirely sure. They days have started to run into each other a little...and with everything going on it didn't occur to me to keep track...over a week maybe."

"Where is the father?" She indicated Cade with a quick slice of her hand.

"Dead," Jessa said, deciding to omit the detail she was the one who killed him.

"I'm so sorry. Did it happen before or after all of this?"

"At the very, very start...I suppose."

"Were you with him when it happened?"

"Yes."

"You were lucky to survive then."

"That pretty much sums it up," Jessa muttered, hoping Sheryl wouldn't ask her to elaborate further.

Sheryl came back with a tray of hot tea and what looked like a fresh loaf of bread and jam.

"Is that...?!" Jessa asked, feeling more excited than she had in days.

"Made today," Sheryl confirmed. "I did a cooking class several years ago. It had seemed kind of pointless at the time considering I've never been much of a cook but they were offering them for free where I work – some kind of health kick I think, wanting us to learn how to make our own bread without preservatives and what not. I ended up enjoying it and it's safe to say it's come in handy now."

"Where did you get the flour?"

"Had it already. And I figured it's not getting any fresher so I might as well use it up."

"How are you baking without electricity though?" Jessa had yet to take her eyes off the fresh bread. She wasn't being particularly polite but all she could think about was getting her hands on it. She *hadn't* been hungry until she was faced with something other than chips, snack-cakes, soda – she had only been trusting pre-packaged stuff because she wasn't sure about use-by-dates.

"Well, for a while I was still able to use my stove because it's gas," Sheryl said. "But that stopped – or got switched off or something – and so I substituted my little Bunsen burner I had left over from when I went camping with my...a few years back." She started speaking very quickly to cover her slight falter but Jessa barely noticed. "Anyway, the bottle still had some gas in it, although I'm sure you can understand it was a very small bottle so I'm not sure how much longer it's going to last but at this point I'm just taking it one day at a time – as no doubt you are too. It's been my saving grace to be able to do some cooking – although it's so much nicer to have someone to cook for. And I don't know what I would do if I couldn't have a cup of tea. Why don't you try some?"

"I've never been that much of a tea drinker," Jessa said. "But I would love some bread!" What she *wanted* to do was dive on it and stuff it all in her mouth and potentially swallow the entire thing whole without chewing. She would probably end up choking and killing herself but what a way to go!

'But this behaviour would not be acceptable in civilized society,' Jessa heard a voice in her head and recognized it as being one of her high-school buddies who had been really good at accents including a fairly decent British one, pretending they were high society. Of course the tasks Kasey used to apply this to were things like drinking straight from the garden hose, mooning people out of the side of a car window or flashing her bra accidentally while changing her shirt in a public place. Kasey being Kasey, this statement usually followed her doing said behaviour and then admitting that it didn't matter because she was in fact, *no* lady.

Thinking about this made Jessa smile, and then frown again when she realized the reality of her friend still being alive. 'Or she's decked herself out like some warrior woman, taking on every Crazy she sees and daring the rest to come after her,' Jessa thought, smiling again.

"What are you thinking?" Sheryl asked, gently tapping her on the shoulder.

"It doesn't matter," Jessa said. "Are you sure you're okay with me eating the bread? I don't won't you to waste all of it on us – particularly since I don't have anything to give you in return."

"No it's fine, you go ahead. There's plenty to go around and it would only go to waste anyway...but you really should try some of the tea..."

2

In the end Jessa did drink a very small cup, if only to appease Sheryl who was being so generous. It had left a bitter after-taste which Jessa tried not to gag on and then waved away any suggestions of another. Happily the sandwiches took away the taste and Jessa ate four slices before she even realized. She had thanked Sheryl but felt like she could already feel the early onset of a food-coma.

'I shouldn't have eaten so much or so quickly,' she thought and gingerly stood up, thinking a little walk around the living room might help to ease the suffering. Cade had also seemed to settle in quite nicely after Sheryl had assured Jessa there was nothing he could hurt himself on and she had let him wander around the living room, trying to keep an eye on him but mostly just monitoring his movements by sound considering the room really was quite shadowy. Fortunately Cade was not a quiet kid so Jessa was easily able to tell where he was.

Jessa considered asking Sheryl some questions – if only because it would be good-mannered but she just felt so tired and full that all she wanted to do was be quiet and rub her belly. Besides, if she was hearing correctly, it sounded like Sheryl was back in the kitchen, humming.

'Glad she's so happy,' Jessa thought, and wondered if the woman seemed strange because she was lonely. 'Maybe Sheryl just needs some company...maybe she'll want to come with us.'

As Jessa considered the possibility of this – it might be good to have someone else around to keep watch or simply help if things took a turn for the worse – she wandered over to a cabinet in the corner, picking up some of the photos and holding them to the light.

'On the other hand, Sheryl seems pretty well set up here, so why would she...' Her thought trailed off as she stared at the photo and tried to understand what was bothering her so much. It was just a basic enough picture: Sheryl holding a newborn baby, looking tired. The baby was screaming and Jessa subconsciously cringed as she thought about the noise it had to have been making.

'Glad I wasn't around to meet you kid,' Jessa thought and then wondered who the child might have been. Jessa put the photo back and picked up another one, this time depicting the same child – or at least she was assuming it was the same child, she couldn't really tell considering all babies pretty much looked alike to her - only this time it was laying in its crib, still screaming.

A third one on a sheep-skin rugs, on its stomach, ass out. Still screaming.

A fourth one in the baby tub. Still screaming.

"*Majorly* glad I didn't have to meet you," Jessa murmured and wondered why on earth Sheryl would have so many photos of this one kid screaming its head off. Feeling uneasy Jessa picked up the lamp and began a slow sweep of the room, taking what she considered a *real* look.

The couch was a couch, nothing unusual about that. Newspapers and magazines piled up on a coffee table, a fine layer of dust over the top of them. Jessa went to read the top covers and see what magazines Sheryl subscribed to but it was as like everything had a hazy tinge to it and she was examining the room through trick binoculars. Her vision had been reduced to a pin-prick with the outer edges out of focus.

The lamp certainly wasn't helping and she considered putting it down since it had grown unexpectedly heavy. 'What the hell is going on?' Jessa wondered and her unease increased several notches.

"Cade?" she called when she realized she could no longer see him. She was fairly certain he was the small dark lump currently half way under the coffee table but couldn't be sure. It could have just as easily been an oversized cat.

'Garfield come to life,' she thought and wanted to laugh even though it wasn't funny. She dropped down on the couch, partly because she wanted to take a closer look at Cade but mostly because it just felt better to be sitting. She found herself staring intently at the edge of the coffee table although she couldn't quite understand what was so important.

'It's got kid-friendly buffering,' she finally realized. They looked styro-foam and protected the edges of fridges or tables when they were moved. They probably had a word for them but Jessa didn't know it.

'Why would Sheryl have these? If they're for that kid in the photos, where's the kid...?'

"Is everything okay in here?" Sheryl softly from behind her.

3

Or at least it sounded soft to Jessa because Sheryl seemed to be standing so far away. She rolled her head to look at her with surprising difficulty and was confused when from this angle it looked like Sheryl's head was brushing the ceiling.

"What happened to the kid?" Jessa asked. Normally she would have tried for a little more tact but everything felt so dreamy and unreal.

There was a look of surprise, pain and maybe even a little shame on Sheryl's face. "How do you know about Leah?"

Trying to say the words "The photographs" for some reason were too much effort so Jessa just kind of waved her hand in the direction of the shelves.

"She was my daughter," Sheryl said, after pausing for so long Jessa had almost fallen asleep.

"Was?" Jessa asked, her mouth barely able to form the word.

"Was."

"How...?" Jessa would have added 'long' but the 'l' was rolling about on her tongue so Sheryl didn't answer the intended question.

"How did she die?" Sheryl asked, glaring at her. "How do you think? How do you think any of us are going to finish up now?! We're going to die screaming and terrified and being ripped apart by those people out there!"

She walked behind the couch where Jessa could no longer see her, pacing back and forth and ranting in a way that would have made Jessa nervous except she was keeping her voice down to a low decibel despite being so on edge.

"We were doing okay – we really were! I got us home and we barricaded the door and like I said, no one really came back after everything started. It's always been just Leah and me anyway so it didn't make that much of a difference! I rationed our food and then when we started to get low, I broke into next-door – they didn't have much because Madeline and Joe practically *live* on take-out...I couldn't figure out how to get into the Thompson's – and then I had this big idea to go downstairs and break into Andrew's place! He's our Super and I figured he must have a master key and that way I could just go through apartment after apartment...but I couldn't get in there, the door wouldn't budge...I even tried breaking in through a high window but I couldn't climb in and only ended up getting myself all scratched up."

She lifted her shirt up to reveal a stomach covered in small swatches of wadding.

"No matter what I did, I couldn't get in – and I was worried about leaving Leah – I had of course left her up here. What kind of mother would I have been if I'd taken her with me?! It hadn't been as bad as it is now but there had still been enough...roaming the streets and...attacking people...and...well...you know."

Jessa *did* know. And she wanted to tell Sheryl to stop because she had a bad feeling she knew where this was going. She didn't know of the *exact* details but was pretty sure this was going to end with a deceased child.

"So I came back and she was still fine – sleeping like a log actually which was pretty unusual considering she'd always been a terrible sleeper from the moment she was born. But we needed food. So I decided we had to go to the big supermarket – it was just two streets over. I thought it was a good idea – it's so close we could walk there and I had been watching the street for hours and hadn't seen anyone – I thought maybe they'd moved on. Found something interesting elsewhere. Pretty stupid, huh? I could have left Leah here but it just freaked me out so much when I'd left her alone for a few minutes while I went downstairs! It usually takes me at least fifteen minutes to walk to store and back – and that's not counting however long it would take me break into the store and get the food. And I would have been even slower coming back ladled down!"

Jessa let her head drop back, closing her eyes and only managing to open them again with great effort.

"I felt like I had no other choice but to take her with me."

"And...bad...happened," Jessa mumbled.

"We got there fine, there was no one else around. The doors were even open so we just walked straight inside...it was a little messy and ransacked but there was still plenty of food left and I grabbed a trolley and just filled up. I also wanted somewhere to put Leah down and have my hands free."

Jessa nodded her head – or at least she thought she did and in her imagination could practically see Sheryl pushing the trolley with Leah in the front, maybe kicking her legs out but otherwise staying quiet and happy for once.

"Everything was fine! And then we rounded a corner and there they were. Maybe it was the smell of the meat that attracted them – it had gone over by now but that doesn't seem to bother them. They didn't notice us until we were right on top of them and even then they only kind of glanced our way."

"So...you...ran."

"I would have if I had been able to move. Instead I was frozen, just watching them eat and there were just so many!...I started walking backwards with the trolley – I'd made sure I picked one that didn't squeak – and we probably would have gotten away except Leah started to cry. I think it was the smell, the spoiled meat stank – and the ones eating it weren't much better Their reaction – it wasn't slow. One minute they were fixed on the meat and the next they were lunging at us. I think I screamed and almost fell down – if I had that would have been the end. But I managed to stay up and didn't even realize I had twisted my ankle until I got home and it ached...I just turned and ran – I got all the way to the end of the aisle before I heard Leah's cries turn into screams and I realized what I'd done – " She raced around to stand in front of Jessa as though needing to make sure she understood the situation.

"I *wanted* to go back for her – I *would* have of course – but it was already too late! There was just no way I could've fought them off! They just would have killed me too!"

'And you wish they had,' Jessa thought, staring into Sheryl's feverish face and wondering how she could have ever trusted her.

"There was *nothing* I could do! Absolutely nothing!...so I just...ran. And her cries...stopped before I even...reached the doors."

"Did...go...back?" Jessa tried to ask. She was pretty sure she must have considering she had all this food but wanted to be sure.

"Yes," Sheryl said, but turned her face away. "I went at night when they were less likely to see me and might mistake me...for one of them. I...I tried...to go down that aisle. The lamp was still glowing – it was one of those special ones that can burn for hours and you can hold it upside down and all sorts of things, I got it from an info-mercial...so I knew which one it was. But I only got as far as the shopping trolley. The food was still inside but the child seat...it was empty, except for...it was empty."

On the one hand Jessa felt outraged – mothers weren't supposed to abandon their children after all – however it seemed like Sheryl was punishing herself enough on her own. Still, Jessa could provide no comfort for her. She had only known Cade for a short while and *certainly* didn't consider herself his mother, yet she wasn't about to forsake him for anything. Even if it meant dying herself.

The silence between them grew until Jessa finally half-heartedly said, "Sorry," and then began the gruelling task of trying to get to her feet to give her a hug. However the minutes she stood up her knees buckled and everything went dark.

Chapter Fifteen –

1

Jessa was still on the couch, although she had fallen over so her head was now on the seat and she was looking at the room on an odd angle. She couldn't tell what time it was thanks to the dark curtains but she could see small swatches of shining sun under the edges of the material where they hadn't been fully stuck down.

She wanted to sit up but her head felt like it had been replaced by an anvil or some other incredible weight that would instantly snap her neck the minute she moved. She tried to groan but all that would come out was a kind of faint whispered sigh that was little more than an expel of air than any real words. Jessa realized she was listening to someone murmuring "Twinkle, Twinkle Little Star".

'That's sweet,' she thought, still half delirious. At this point she was happy to handover the comforting duties to someone else for a little while since she felt so bad. She hadn't heard Cade fuss and hoped he didn't cause too much trouble for Sheryl while Jessa's own head felt so fuzzy. The song ended and was replaced by Sheryl's gentle murmuring instead.

"You are just the sweetest little thing in the world, aren't you baby? I'm going to take such good care of you – you don't have to worry. You don't have to worry about anything ever again! Everything's going to be alright and I'm never ever going to leave you alone again."

On top of her already extreme and unexpected symptoms, Jessa now felt sweaty as she tried to focus closer on what was being said.

"I'm so sorry about last time, okay? Mummy is so very, very sorry. But it's going to be okay now because I'm going to do better. I'm not going to make the same mistakes. And look! I kept all of your toys and everything is still here, waiting! We're going to be happy now and I'll make your 'special food' whenever you want and I'll be more careful and keep you safe and protect you. Okay baby? Okay my sweet, sweet baby? I love you so very much!"

Jessa tried to argue this was all a pretend game of Sheryl's. That the woman hadn't *really* lost her mind and *did* understand Cade wasn't her deceased daughter. That she was just 'working through her issues' by play-acting or whatever – that Cade was a living, breathing, (no doubt squirming) embodiment of that. However her rolling stomach already knew better.

'She drugged me...she wants Cade...'

Jessa had no idea why she was still alive – maybe she hadn't drunk as much of the offered tea as Sheryl realized. Cade also didn't seem to be as accepting of Sheryl's singing or her attempts at soothing him either. Maybe he sensed that the other woman's sanity had well and truly cracked and knew it was only going to be a matter of time before she began to dress him like a girl, tell him he *was* a girl, hell, maybe this was the kind of shit that only happened in Days of our lives-type movies, but Jessa had witnessed so many things lately that fell into the realm of fantasy that *anything* seemed possible. Thus Jessa could easily imagine one night Sheryl laying Cade out on the kitchen table and castrating the poor kid just so she could continue to hold on to her mad-capped beliefs.

'I have to protect him!'

Unfortunately just because she knew this *didn't* mean she *could*. Jessa tried to push herself off the couch and instead only succeed in sort of flopping onto the carpet, her body making a slight thumping sound as she landed. She couldn't even cry out in pain although it felt like her brain had become dislodged and someone was bouncing it up and down like a basketball within her skull.

She could have stayed like that for a while, just experiencing the sensation of her blood coursing through her body and half wishing it would stop even if that meant her death but a hardened part of her knew time was wasting and if she was in pain, she might as well embrace it and keep going.

She got onto her knees, one hand on her head to help hold it up and the other on the coffee table for leverage. She managed to stand but needed to hold on to the back of the couch in order to remain upright, grabbing the TV remote off the table without thinking and flinging it in Sheryl's direction.

It didn't hit her but instead crashed into the wall directly behind. She jumped at the sudden crash and automatically ducked, shielding Cade even as he thrashed and tried to get away from her.

'Maybe the kid has his own intuition lady,' Jessa thought and threw her body up and then forward, hoping her momentum would help.

Luckily Sheryl wasn't that far away and due to weight and age she was slow moving. She just had time to glance at the now broken remote on the floor and then turn in the direction of where it had come from, a strange sort of "Wha-omph?" sound coming out of her mouth as Jessa tried to tackle her to the floor.

Maybe it was her overall size that helped Sheryl to stay upright even as Jessa hit her target and tried to ride her to the floor but for a few moments they hung in the balance as Sheryl fought and probably could have easily bucked Jessa off except Jessa grabbed Sheryl's hair as she went down, pulling her body back and exposing her throat.

Jessa pulled with everything she had and wasn't at all surprised when she thought she felt something in her *own* back pull and wrench as she used muscles she had only ever felt once in a phys ed. class when their teacher had decided they were going to give archery a try. It worked though and as Sheryl fell back, Cade was dropped too, landing on the carpet and almost instantly rolling to his side. Jessa pulled on Sheryl a little bit extra, making sure they landed to the left of Cade and then held on fast to Sheryl's hair while the other one went around her neck.

"You thought you could do this to *me*?!" Jessa tried to say aloud but the words only came out garbled. She couldn't tell if it was the effect of whatever Sheryl had given her or just her own rage over-powering her ability to create speech. "What did you think I was?!" Jessa continued even though it was probably still garbled nonsense to Sheryl. "Just some idiot so you could take whatever the hell you wanted?! Did you think it would be that easy?! Why the hell would you be better than me after what you did to your own?!"

With each point made Jessa used Sheryl's hair to bash her head into the floor. Unfortunately the thickness of the carpet meant she wasn't doing half as much damage as she wanted to and with a growl of frustration, Jessa's hand reached for something else – anything nearby – her hand closing around a chair leg.

Jessa squeezed with her knees on Sheryl's ribs and then one handed dragged the dining chair towards her. She didn't even think about it as one minute she was sitting on Sheryl's back and the next she was up standing, nothing but white noise in her ears, drowning out both Cade's cries and Sheryl's own groans at having been treated so unexpectedly poorly.

The chair felt like it weighed nothing as Jessa brought it down with as much force as she could muster, one chair leg hitting Sheryl's head and the other the floor with such speed it almost bounced back up again to hit Jessa in the face. She flinched away but there was nothing that was going to divert her from her task.

With the second blow she made sure it was *Sheryl* this time who experienced the sharp edge of the chair leg and the blow was accompanied with a fine spray of blood and a damp, coppery smell. The chair bounced up yet again and Jessa brought it down for a third and then a fourth time.

There was a squelching sensation reverberating from the chair hitting its target and then pulling it back up again. It felt to Jessa like she smashing into a pie or some other kind of cream filled pastry and all the innards were sucking on the chair. And in that moment her mind shut off all other thoughts and everything went dark again as Jessa fainted.

Chapter Sixteen –

1

Jessa didn't know if she passed out as a result of her body still trying to fight off the drugs on top of the exertion of the fight or if she had actually fainted upon realizing what she had just done. She guessed it didn't matter as she was roused by the sound of Cade's crying.

"Leah?" Jessa said blearily, thoroughly confused. She didn't even understand why she said this name and in that moment, didn't remember who Leah was. The room was dark but there were still small bars of light getting through under the curtains. Jessa had landed on her back on the carpet and it was as though the more awake she became, the less she understood. She should have been in bed, thinking about what food she was going to get for the party tonight that she was having with her housemates.

'But Elle's dead,' she reminded herself. 'Just like Tez and at least one of his girlfriends...they're all dead and Sam is gone...he left with his mother and his crazy brother.'

It was as though this was something Jessa knew academically but she couldn't understand what it *meant*.

Jessa *knew* that something bad had happened. She *knew* the crying she heard was probably Cade. She *knew* her name was Jessa and that she had been hurt in some way, but now – with the exception of the raging headache that might have been just as much a product of sleeping on the floor or the kid's crying – she was doing okay.

She rolled over and got to all fours, moving slowly and carefully.

"It's okay Cade," she called out. "I'm here."

Even though it probably would have been a quicker trip to go around the back of the couch to get to him, Jessa automatically went the long way, crawling on her hands and knees, coming in from the side and reaching for him.

She couldn't see too well in the dim twilight of the room but could tell Cade was borderline hysterical, almost choking on his back, his face a mess of tears and snot. Jessa tugged him towards her. "Come on," she said. "Come here little buddy."

He howled even louder but also slowly crawled towards her and plopped down in her lap, paradoxically his crying actually increasing.

"It's okay Cade," she said over and over. "It's okay, I'm here now. You're going to be fine."

2

It would have made more sense if they had stayed there. But instead Jessa put her arms around Cade and lifted him up, ignoring the shaking in her legs and how being upright left her feel like she was trying to balance on stilts. In fact this sensation was so strong she actually reached up for the ceiling to steady herself, surprised when she couldn't reach it. She went for the front door, getting her coat on one-handed and then closing it around the pair of them. It wasn't ideal but had the added bonus of muffling Cade's cries which Jessa felt was important for some reason.

Her bag was more troublesome to wrestle on – to the point of where she actually considered leaving it behind and just getting the hell out of there. There was something wrong about this place. Shadows everywhere so it felt haunted and she thought there was even moaning coming from the corner although that had to be her imagination.

Jessa didn't close the door behind her when she went out. She just walked in a daze past several other yawning doorways and then down the staircase and away. Away was important. Away was good.

The daylight was blinding once she got outside. It felt a little like she was exiting a cave after several months of hibernation, the sun hurting her eyes but the air was fresh and wide open space welcoming. Out here the quiet didn't seem quite as oppressive. Hell, she almost thought she could hear some birds twittering and seriously, how terrible could things be if there were birds twittering?

Jessa didn't have a destination in mind and merely picked a direction based on the breeze – she wanted it blowing in her face rather than whipping her hair forward. She started off walking on the path, moving to the road when the way became blocked with rubbish and what looked like bundles of cloth that could have been in the shape of something she recognized but Jessa refused to examine.

By chance she picked the route which took them straight towards a little park with a small playground, fenced all around with a swing set, slide and small jungle gym.

'Leah must have loved coming here,' Jessa thought and again pushed this away so suddenly it was almost a physical jerk from her body.

She found the small gate parents unlocked to get inside and made sure to close it behind her, not certain why she was making such a big deal considering the fence was only about waist-high and therefore easily jumped over but because it seemed like the thing to do.

She found a bench that had a good view of the playground and gently lowered Cade on to the wooden slats before dropping down herself. It was no great surprise though when Cade didn't last long sitting there. Instead he almost immediately wriggled around until he was on his stomach and lowered himself to the ground.

Jessa merely watched him struggle and then toddle off on his little legs towards the sandpit, wondering briefly about the things kids found in sandpits these days, but then deciding that out of all the dangers that existed for them these days, *that* was the least of them. She kept waiting to hear the sounds of a Crazy spotting them and running over – after all there had certainly been enough of them before – and she couldn't understand where they had all gone. Even Sheryl's story had involved mobs of them swarming the area – and then just like that, all the numbness Jessa had been striving so hard to hold onto, dissolved.

She felt an invisible vice suddenly close in around her chest and throat, squeezing so hard she felt the pressure in her eyes and wondered if it really was possible for them to pop out and for the inside of her skull to leak out like someone squeezing a toothpaste tube from the middle. She couldn't breathe but that was okay because she didn't want to. It felt better not to breathe because then she didn't have to keep going. Her vision started to go dark around the edges and that was okay and welcome.

'I'll just lay down,' she thought. 'And then maybe a Crazy will come along and I won't wake up again...that would be good.'

It would be easy. So much easier than this. The world had gone to hell and what was she really hanging on for anyway? Her mother wasn't going to be there waiting for her. She was just going to find her dead body – or worse than that, no body at all. Then she would have to constantly wonder where her mother was and what had happened to her and if she was actually somewhere very, very close, waiting for rescue or she had become crazy too. And if they *did* manage to find each other, she would run to embrace her mother and her mother would –

Jessa felt something touch her hand – it almost felt like the wet nose of a puppy – accompanied by a slight tugging.

"Mama," Cade said in a sing-song voice.

Jessa's felt her heart rate sky-rocketed as her first ridiculous thought was that Cade's mother had somehow found them. That impossible miracles and coincidences like this could happen in this new peculiar reality.

"Mama," Cade tried again.

And now the kid wanted Jessa to come meet her so they could all be friends and the mother could thank Jessa for taking such good care of her kid but that she would now take over –

Cade patted her face, saying "Mama" over and over again, giggling at first as though this was a game and then with more insistence when Jessa didn't respond. His voice was far away, easy to ignore. Someone else's problem. Someone else could deal with it. It didn't matter –

Jessa opened her eyes. It wasn't a sudden movement and neither was the deep breath she took. The vice was still squeezing her body but she sat up and looked down at the kid.

He continued to watch her with his big eyes and Jessa just stared back, waiting and hoping for some kind of surge of energy or positive emotion to overwhelm her and leave her able to persist.

But there was none of that.

It was just Cade staring at her, one of his little hands on her knee using it to balance, seemingly waiting for her to decide.

Her thoughts tried to go to her mother again but that proved too painful. It briefly tried to examine what she had done to Sheryl but that too was a topic she couldn't dwell on. And finally all that was left was remembering Cade's father. The man she had met what felt like in another life who had helped her reach a high packet of chips and who had ended up entrusting his son to some stupid girl he didn't know from Adam.

"I didn't ask for you," she said to Cade. "But you didn't ask for me either. I'm sorry kid."

If she was expecting some deep words or advice to suddenly come from him like he had become Yoda or the embodiment of Buddha, then she was sorely mistaken. Cade only continued to rub his hand back and forth on her pants and Jessa slowly realized it was that the material they were made of probably felt nice to touch. Feeling more tired than she had ever, Jessa climbed to her feet, stooping down to pick up Cade, and then start walking again.

Chapter Seventeen –

1

Jessa decided she'd had enough of people for a while.

"My kingdom for a little loneliness, eh Cade?" she muttered. With his ruling consent Jessa had forgone the cities and their maze of streets and entered suburbia where it should have been safer and quieter.

Besides, she had started to come across barriers and traps in some places in the city. Usually situated between two buildings – large chain-link fences that at first looked like walls created to keep people out and those inside safe but then as Jessa walked around them and saw how they had been placed, she realized they were more like cages.

She taken a closer look at some of the bodies trapped inside, some morbid part of her wanting to see if their heads were continuing to move even after their vital organs had been disintegrated.

Some had been dressed like Jessa, ready for the elements and like they were in the middle of a hike; and others who had taken advantage of all rules going out the window, seizing the opportunity to do something they had probably dreamt about their whole lives. *They* were dressed to the nines, dripping in jewels and fur coats, expensive leather coats and other things that were in no way practical – but lavish.

Jessa had stared at an entire pen of them.

'The Crazies didn't do this,' she thought. They Crazies killed and ripped people to shreds but they didn't bother with traps – or use weapons for that matter!

So regular people who were still okay had done it.

And these weren't the only traps either.

At first it felt like she had somehow been transported to the medieval times where people were tied to poles and left to starve and for birds to peck out their eyes. In the movies these people were usually skeletons wearing raggedy ends of clothes and so were rarely – if ever – distressing. However these ones were nowhere *near* that stage yet.

Some were in proper cages, possibly meant for housing large dogs like at the vet, but others were cobbled together bits of wood and chicken wire. These ones were a lot harder to see into and usually only had one or two small 'windows' and while Jessa was curious to see what was inside, the smell emanating from them were generally enough to drive her away.

None of them had obvious signs of death-inducing injuries though – self-inflicted ones sure, usually self-cannibalism by the looks – which of course made Jessa think about the Crazies and wondering what *they* did when they couldn't find anything to eat. But these people were still all wearing the same 'travel uniform' of regular people fleeing. And then she started to see signs set up under each one.

They were only pieces of cardboard sometimes tied to the cages or placed around the necks of the victims themselves, but they were each written thickly and clearly in black paint. Traitor. Thief. Or the simple but far more ominous: Unworthy.

It was these messages that sent shivers down her spine – almost as much as the Crazies did as she wondered *who* exactly was making these judgements.

2

'This will never be over, will it?' Jessa wondered bitterly. She didn't know how long it was going to be before her own mind cracked and she began to consider it a good idea to hang people's heads from lampposts or firebomb anyone who looked even remotely humanoid –

The woman hadn't looked up when Jessa came towards her. She looked to be in her fifties, dressed in an oversized tan jacket with a sheepskin lining and a hood that had pooled forward from the woman's head resting on her chest.

Jessa didn't really want to look but at the same time, couldn't turn away as she stared at the woman's outstretched legs and arms that had been tied to posts in an X-formation.

'She's been crucified,' Jessa thought, taking another step forward.

The woman's face was dirt-stained and there was a cut on one side with dried blood running down her cheek and a purple bruise. Maybe she –

The woman suddenly gasped and Jessa's heart beat so fast she was sure if she looked down she would see a small lump thumping under her skin, possibly bumping Cade in the face. The woman's head slowly rose and she looked at Jessa with her one good eye – the other was sort of bulging from the eye-socket.

"Help me," she gasped, speaking as though she was either a very heavy smoker or had recently spent a great deal of time screaming. "Please help me! Water...please!" The woman's her head fell forward again and Jessa dropped down to one knee and rummaged in the front of her backpack, pulling out a half-filled bottle. She put her hand gently under her chin and lifted. The woman took the smallest of sips and then coughed most of it out anyway.

"Who did this to you?" Jessa asked.

"Bad...bad people...please help me!"

"Where did they go?"

Every word seemed to need a great deal of effort for the woman but Jessa persevered.

"There was...a woman...she was...watching over me until the others came back."

"What woman?"

"She heard a noise...and went away...more water..."

Jessa gave her another sip, this one seemingly going down a lot better. "Who are the others?"

"I don't know – I..."

"How many of them are there?"

"A few....please – can you – "

"Were you travelling with anyone?" Jessa gently pushed some of the woman's hair out of her eyes and gently held her hand against the woman's feverish cheek.

"Yes." She looked like she wanted to cry but possibly because of her injuries, wasn't able to manage it.

"What happened to them?"

"They killed them. But I think a few of the others managed to get away. I made the mistake of coming back though – my son, he was one of the ones shot only I wasn't sure...I just had to come back to make sure...I had to know he was...if he was here."

Jessa started to ask if he was but changed her mind since it probably didn't matter.

"That hag was waiting for me. I think they left her behind to keep watch just in case."

"And she did this to you?"

"Yes. Please help me get free!"

If Jessa had thought it was possible she would have untied the woman and maybe even helped her get a few streets away before leaving her to her own fate. Unfortunately being up this close she could see the woman was tied to the posts using those plastic ties and around her one of her legs was an actual a set of handcuffs.

"Please – before they come back!"

Jessa felt a sensation similar to an ice-cube being run down her spine.

"That's where she probably went – to get the others! Please don't leave me like this – they're gonna kill – hey, where are you going?!"

'Don't turn around,' Jessa repeated over and over in her head. 'Don't turn around. Just keep going and pretending you don't hear her. She's nothing. She's a ghost who doesn't exist. She – '

"No please – you can't do this! You don't know what they will do to me! Please it hurts so bad! I'm a person – my name is Rebecca – *please*!"

The woman's pleas got louder and louder – certainly not on the same level as a shout, she didn't have enough voice left for that – but there was still a raspy desperation that made Jessa feel even more like she was talking to a spectre trying to remain in the land of the living but who's grip was getting looser and looser.

'That's right, she's dead already. You're not leaving her to die. Look at her – she wouldn't last a day without a doctor and there's nothing you can do – '

"I'll tell them you were here!"

Jessa halted in her tracks, wanting to make sure she'd heard right.

"I'll tell them you were here and which way you went."

Jessa turned around slowly to stare at her and while the expression on the woman's face held a little guilt, it also held a great deal of defiance.

"I have a kid," Jessa said. She genuinely wasn't using Cade as an excuse that they should be left alone but more that even in this world of complete lawlessness, it was imperative to look after the children – especially since the woman had been a mother too.

"I'm sorry...I don't want to...but *please*, you can't just leave me here! I won't let you!"

"They'll hurt him if you do this. They'll find us and he'll be strung up right next to you," Jessa was saying as much to the woman as herself.

"It doesn't have to be that way! Just get me down and we can help each other!"

"I don't have any bolt cutters," Jessa said, her mouth almost talking independently of what the woman was saying. "How am I supposed to help you?"

She put Cade down gently on the curb of the street, slipping off her jacket to wrap around him.

"My knife!" the woman said, pointing with the few remaining unbroken fingers on her left hand. "It's down there! They...used it on me a little."

Jessa glanced down at a blade that probably would have glinted in the light given the overall size of the blade but which was currently dull with blood and thus, almost hidden amongst the other tools such as a hammer and what looked a little like a rusted saw blade.

"You just need to saw through the cuffs and ties! – quick please! – we don't know how long they'll be!"

Jessa spotted an axe mixed in with everything else and even though she knew a knife would probably be easier, she was hoping an axe would make it quick. She was surprised by the weight but still thought she could swing it without difficulty.

The woman's eyes widened at Jessa's choice of implements but she kept her mouth shut. Jessa too had decided the time for talking strategy had passed.

She hefted the axe over one shoulder, grateful the woman had opted to shut her eyes – well, she shut one of her eyes and the other one wasn't really looking at Jessa anyway – as they both braced themselves.

Jessa let fly with all the strength she could muster, taking special notice of the sensation of the swinging axe and not what was going to come next. It was almost like she was a kid playing batter-up and any minute now she was going to feel the bat connect with the ball and –

She suddenly did feel the axe 'connect', the sensation of entering and then slowly sinking – like a knife in butter. The momentum meant it would only go so far but the slowing down was soft and let her know it was now stuck.

Sure enough, when Jessa opened her eyes again the axe was buried deep in the woman's skull, not directly down the middle of her head but at a slight angle so it had gone in through the top, slicing between her eyes. Her nose was still attached to her 'good' eye but the rest was off to the side. It kind of looked like she had tried to do some kind of half-assed operation on the woman, wanting to remove the 'broken' portion of her face.

Jessa stared at what she had done, feeling numb. There was nothing else that could have been done. There was no way she could have sawn through those cuffs – it would have taken ages and as it was, she wasn't entirely sure how much longer she could waste standing there, staring.

The woman would have told them which way they had gone – she would have set these people straight onto her and Cade if it had meant giving herself a little bit longer to live.

The woman suddenly – and impossibly – gasped, her one remaining eye grew impossibly wide and not exactly staring at her would-be killer, but more *through* her. Jessa took an automatic step backwards, hoping this was just the woman's final death gasp, however she continued staring and breathing.

'I should put her out of her misery,' Jessa thought, but then remembered the sensation of the axe sinking into her skull and how it was probably going to take some wrenching to get free. Just imagining doing this was enough and Jessa spun to her left, doubled over with her hands on her knees and threw up everything in her stomach and then continued to dry heave for several more minutes.

'They're going to know I was here now...and the woman with an axe buried in her head wasn't going to be enough of a clue?!'

Sarcasm – sarcasm was good. Sarcasm was Jessa's friend and made her feel like she was still a human being despite everything. She straightened up less because she needed to and more because being bent over was making her head throb. Her throat already burned but at least her stomach was no longer cramping.

She grasped the end of a nearby cardboard box and put it over the mess she had made. The fluid soaked through quickly, leaving a wet stain in the middle but the stain could have come from rain or something wet in the garbage.

'Maybe I should take the axe with me,' Jessa thought, not noticing a fine tremor had begun in her body. Her vision started to blur around the edges, making her surroundings shapeless and unrecognizable. She kept her eyes straight ahead, not really seeing anything and pausing only to pick up the warm, shapeless lump she hoped was Cade, grateful he still seemed asleep.

Chapter Eighteen –

1

Jessa wanted to sit down.

She wanted a hot cup of coffee, to turn on the TV and watch cartoons or something equally as childish which wouldn't require her to think or do anything other than let the boob-tube work its will.

She wanted a hot shower – or a bath with so many bubbles they spilled over the edge. To wash her hair and dry herself with one of the fluffiest towels ever created, put on some fresh clothes that had just come in off the line maybe put on some perfume and moisturiser – and sit down.

She wanted to get into a kitchen and make two trays of extra chocolate-chip brownies, order a pizza dripping with cheese and sit down.

She wanted to take the knapsack off her back, the kid off her chest and sit down.

Holy hell, did she want to sit down.

At least one good thing about all this walking was that she was feeling better in her head. She had walked in a daze for the rest of the previous night, occasionally feeling like she heard voices crying out in anger and frustration behind her, howling at the moon like Crazies only they still had their cunning. But Jessa had told herself it was just the wind – or even *actual* animals! She hadn't seen too many of them and had been under the impression they were just as much a target for the Crazies as people were but maybe animals were reverting back to their former selves too. Becoming just as savage as nature originally intended and fighting back.

There had been a car that had come tearing down the road and out of the darkness, no headlights but the roar of the engine unmissable in the otherwise quiet. Jessa had stopped and listened for several seconds trying to figure out where it was coming from and exactly how far away it was and then it was suddenly around the bend. She barely had time to throw herself off the road and dive to the grass to avoid getting hit. She had then lain in the grass for several minutes, listening to the car revving and getting further and further away.

An overwhelming weariness had hit her and it had seemed pointless to go any further. Cade had stayed quiet during her leap to the grass, even though he must have been jolted too. His only reaction had been to snuffle slightly and then bat at her chest – not like he was trying to reproach her, but more one of those involuntary movements people did in their sleep.

Jessa had crawled on her hands and knees among the grass, too weary to even stand and with her concentration solely on the ground, almost banged her head into a tree.

It wasn't a large one but had several low hanging branches which Jessa had crawled under, tucking her body into a small ball and resting under the shelter it provided.

She had woken in the morning, more than a little confused and feeling a little like the first time she had gotten drunk, consuming so much alcohol she had blacked out and come to on the couch with no recollection of where she was or how she had gotten there.

'What the hell was I thinking?' Jessa had asked herself but she knew the answer already: she *hadn't* been thinking.

All the reasons why she shouldn't have done this – all the dangers she had risked – had dropped on her like a weight and she'd felt all of her muscles constrict painfully as she had no choice but to let the extreme fear to flood in and hopefully leave her still able to function again on the other side.

'Cade – where's Cade! Anything could have come for – all night alone – out in the cold – those bad people could be searching – !' Jessa had finally taken a great lungful of air and then gagged, falling against the tree but now able to see Cade had not disappeared – he had just rolled over in his sleep but still been doing okay wrapped in her jacket.

"Still, let's not do that again," she had muttered, noting she had collapsed somewhere in the middle of a field, the bare-stick tree providing some basic shelter as –

Jessa had jerked suddenly when she heard a sound behind them and realized it was a Crazy, trying to get to them from the other side. Rather than walk around it, this one had decided the quickest route was *through* the tree. It had been reaching for them but the thickness of the branches had kept it at bay and Jessa's teeth had come together with a clang when she realized she had no idea how long it had been there, trying to get at them and what would have happened if it had finally worked out to come around the front and fall on them.

It had reeked to high heaven, with a coating across its eyes and gunk oozing from a neck wound may have once been blood but was now a thick, black discharge that had a slight greenish tinge. Gender wise it had maybe been a male, his skin covered in sores, growling and reaching for her almost blindly – 'Does it have a sense of smell?' Jessa had wondered. 'Is *that* how it knows where we are?' – and there had really no denying it anymore. It had been dead.

"Shit," Jessa had muttered under her breath and then scrambled away, scratching her face on one of the branches, practically impaling herself in her haste to put some distance between it and them. She had left Cade where he was, still half under the tree and half out and climbed to her feet, never once taking her eyes off their uninvited visitor. She had broken off one of the branches of the tree – it hadn't been very long or heavy but as Jessa had started leading the dead thing away, she had been able to wield like a baseball bat, ready to swing it with everything she had in the hopes of separating the Crazie's head from its body.

Jessa didn't want to think too hard back on the fight – the thing had temporarily rode her down after she had made the mistake of trying to wrestle with it – but once she jammed the stick into the roof of its mouth and then further and further into its skull and whatever had been left that counted as a brain, it had grown still and she had pushed it off.

Jessa had then grabbed Cade and started walking again, more vigilant than ever.

However as it turned out they hadn't come through that night's stupidity as unscathed as she dared to hope.

Cade had finally woken up with a sniffle that had then become a wheezing cough and Jessa had no longer felt any kind of need for her jacket because she essentially now had the equivalent of a hot-water-bottle strapped to her chest.

Cade had grizzled for the rest of the day – first he wanted to be held, then he wanted to be put down; he wanted to walk, he wanted to be carried; he wanted to eat, he pushed it away. Jessa couldn't blame him too much for any of this – if she had been sick she doubted she would have been all that pleasant either. And then of course there was the added consideration that she was the *reason* he was sick.

She knew they needed to find some place to hold up for a while and stop travelling but her safety fears had sky-rocketed. With her caution levels at an all-time high she just kept picturing whoever had been in that car still searching for them, possibly even doing it strategically in every little hidey-hole and shelter they came to – including houses, other cars, public toilets at the park where Jessa had wasted several moments contemplating resting in once it had started to rain.

Eventually she had concluded it wasn't going to be safe again until she was in the next town.

Which was no doubt why she was feeling so incredibly tired now and why she was mumbling almost incoherently to Cade. She wasn't sick herself but wondered if it was only a matter of time.

"We'll get you some kid-aspirin or something. And then you'll feel a lot better." Jessa leaned back slightly so she could put her hand on Cade's forehead and wasn't at all surprised to find it dripping with sweat.

"Maybe I should give you a bath," Jessa said. "Wash you down or something...or get my hands on one of those books – 'What to expect when you're expecting', only for toddlers or whatever. There's got to be a couple of those around, explaining to new-mothers what they're meant to do...unlike screwing up *royally* like I've done. Bet you're wishing your Dad found someone else right about now. Someone who had a clue would be nice, eh? Hell, maybe you would have been better off with that Sheryl – she might have renamed you Leah but she probably wouldn't have let you get sick..."

Cade stirred slightly and a part of Jessa wanted him to wake-up and give her a sign of life, while another part just wanted him to continue to get the rest he so obviously needed. Cade's eyes fluttered briefly and he tried to grab at the shirt on her chest but his grip was weak and Jessa's fear increased.

"Okay kid," she said. "It's rallying time again. Time to stop with all this self-pitying nonsense."

Jessa had spotted a two-story, mansion type-house up on a hill about an hour ago, watching it get bigger as they go closer. It was hard to miss given its size, three stories and painted white with dark blue, manicured lawn and perfect garden bed. To Jessa it very much resembled a display home.

Most of the other houses she had passed on her trek had otherwise shown obvious signs that something had gone wrong. Indications of either people packing up and leaving in a hurry; of Crazies managing to get inside and attack the previous occupants. However this house showed none of that. There was no destruction or blood anywhere – hell, not even a blade of grass looked out of place.

"Maybe it's a mirage." Jessa wasn't sure how much of this was a joke considering while she didn't *feel* sick, that didn't mean she couldn't still be delirious from exhaustion.

She approached slowly, ready to run the moment anything so much as twitched but also because the house was at the top of what was probably a very gentle rise but in her current state, might as well have been Mount Everest.

'Just keep putting one foot in front of the other,' she advised herself. 'Don't think about anything else beyond just the next step.'

By the time she reached the door she would have happily dropped to her knees and collapsed right there except she had learnt the hard way that she no longer had that luxury.

She put her back to the outside wall and peered in the windows. She didn't know why she was being stealthy – it didn't seem like anyone was home and besides, if they were watching they would have seen her coming up the lawn – but it seemed the thing to do.

Looking inside everything looked neat and tidy, although she realized she was able to look in one window, through the house and then into the backyard on the other side due to a complete lack of curtains. This increased her feeling that this was a display home full of beautiful furniture but where the dressers invariably forgot certain details such as dishes in the cupboards, sheets on the beds – and curtains in the windows.

She went to the front door and was only mildly surprised to find it locked and so began circling for an open window or other way to gain entry, finally eyeing the doggy-door critically.

'Absolutely no chance,' she decided after coming up with the mental image of her getting stuck. Cade might have been able to squeeze through but in all likelihood she would get trapped around her hips and be stuck there until one of the dead ones came along and bit her in the ass.

"That would just be the perfect ending to all of this, wouldn't it Cade?" she muttered, automatically giving the door knob a few twists to verify it was locked too. No magical pixie had come along to unlock it for them so Jessa was left with the window over the kitchen sink.

"Eureka," she said under her breath, perched ridiculously on the edge of bin trying to balance without falling off – or falling in – while working her fingers under the small crack of the window which had been left open. 'I should just break a window to get in,' she thought but she was already half way through and after a particularly vigorous shove, toppled head first onto the kitchen floor.

"That certainly was a whole 'three-stooges' moment, wasn't it Cade?" she told him when she retrieved him from the stoop, reclosing the window behind her but not securing it because she could now see the lock had been broken.

2

As expected it was all just so incredibly clean, making Jessa feel guilty because she and Cade were so grotty.

"Pretty silly, eh Cade?" she said. "But I almost don't even want to sit down in here!"

The couches in the lounge weren't completely white, but white with dark blue stripes, possibly the inspiration for – or maybe even the cause of – the nautical theme used throughout the room.

"Whoever designed the interior of this house had *money*," Jessa said as she took Cade from room to room, partially wanting to check the security and partially just check everything *out*.

There was a grand piano big enough that it could have doubled as a queen-sized bed, a dining table – in fact a whole other dining *room* – which threw Jessa a little considering she and her mother usually ate in their kitchen and in the share house a person had been lucky if they made it further than the kitchen sink. The table in *this* house however had sixteen place-settings, all set-up ready for a fancy dinner.

She found two separate bathrooms just on the downstairs floor – both empty with the exception of toilet paper and fancy, shaped soaps ('They remembered soaps but forgot *toilet paper*?!'). A study as neat as a pin and just waiting for some old professor guy to sit behind the desk and light up a pipe. And then a garage that had no windows and no obvious light-switch so she didn't know what *it* contained and pushed a small table against the door, hoping that would be enough.

The upstairs of the house had a slightly more 'lived-in' feel oddly. Once again every one of the five bedrooms was spick and span, beds made, everything put away and perfect and ready-to buy and move in. But there were a few more subtle details – a movie poster on the wall, soft toys looking les then pristine lined up on a shelf.

Each room had a queen-sized bed though – even the little kid's one – and then the Master that contained a bed so big Jessa didn't even know what to class it as. It looked like it could have slept up to five adults side by side, easily.

'This has to be a display home, then,' Jessa thought. 'No regular person would need a bed so big. Some developer picked it 'cause they thought it would impress potential buyers.' A dressing gown had even been draped across the end as though waiting for the owner to come home and get all snuggly.

Jessa found herself staring at this piece of material for several moments. It was just so clean and luxurious and out of place in terms of what her world had become. She wanted to touch the satin but at the same time, didn't want to mess with the scene. She crossed the large expanse to one of two closed doors, guessing that one would either be the walk-in-robe that would no doubt accompany a room as extravagant as this or the en-suite bathroom that was just as obligatory. Jessa was mildly interested in finding out what size of a wardrobe would go with this room – 'Probably something the size of my whole bedroom back at the share house,' she surmised – and was also expecting it to seem even bigger considering it would be empty –

"I may be wrong, Cade," she said to the unconscious child. "Either that or the hired set-dresser really went all out!"

The wardrobe wasn't quite as big as she had imagined – or maybe it was just the reverse of what she had been thinking before – it *was* big but didn't seem so because it was absolutely choc-full of clothes, shoes, coats and bags. Jessa almost didn't want to step inside because she was afraid she would get claustrophobic as the collection reached all the way up to the already high ceiling and filled every available space to capacity, ready and waiting to bury her if she touched the wrong thing.

'Whoever neatens and organizes the rest of the house certainly doesn't have anything to do with *this* wardrobe.' She saw an open space at the very, very back, flashing bright compared to the darkness created by all these possessions but she still double-checked the second door, just to make sure she was right. This wardrobe opened up on a regular-sized closet, nowhere near as full and containing what looked like just fancy suits and tuxedos and a snow suit.

'Husband's closet,' Jessa thought. 'Or just the one too small to be of any use to the *lady of the house*.'

Even though it didn't make sense, Jessa had taken an instant dislike to the woman who obviously lived here. Jessa's previous life hadn't exactly been Spartan to begin with but life on the road had done a great deal to change her views on useless clutter and 'status possessions'.

"There's probably four or five cars down in that garage too, Cade," she said. "And maybe even a boat or a jet ski. How ridiculous, eh?"

Ridiculous or not, Jessa was hoping that for a pack-rat such as this, she might also have a bathroom just as fully and completely stocked. Make-up and all the latest beauty products for sure but maybe also someone deeply unhappy and therefore, self-medicating.

"See Cade, that's text-book pop-psychology. When you feel like something is missing inside, you have a tendency to fill your surroundings as much as possible."

The woman of the house might have been on a slippery-slope but the bathroom was as spic and span as downstairs. Blindingly white tiles, a bathtub that could have doubled as a small swimming pool, what looked like a *three*-person shower and even one of those fancy, round couch things that Jessa had only seen before in movies set in the thirties or in hotel lobbies. It was cream to match the tiles and Jessa had no idea why someone would put such a thing in a bathroom.

Almost every wall had a mirror which created a fun-house effect – although there was nothing *fun* about it. Jessa had never been a big fan of the mirror-mazes to begin with and seeing herself duplicated until there were about twenty versions would have been bad enough on its own except currently she looked like hell.

She was pale with dark circles under her eyes so she resembled one of those zombies from the original 'Night of the Living Dead' movies. Her hair was dirty and matted and there was a smear of mud on her cheek, possibly from her impromptu night spent sleeping outside. Her clothes were smelly and she looked as grungy as she felt, her expression worn out and shell-shocked.

"Haggard," her reflections told her. "You look haggard Jessa-baby."

It was almost possible to believe the person in the mirror had absolutely nothing to do with her. Sure, there was a passing resemblance but that was all she had in common with this barely alive creature! If there had been just one mirror than she would have been able to turn her back on it and kept it catalogued in the back of her mind with everything else she didn't want to deal with. However everywhere she turned there was another one and then another. A whole army of Jessa's all looking like they were wondering what had happened to her young, carefree self of only a couple of weeks ago.

'When my biggest concern had been how long I could procrastinate on an essay or cleaning the bathroom before the mould infestation became a serious problem.'

Jessa looked down at the tiles and her shoes – not very practical but better than trying to equate the person in the mirror with her own mental image of herself – and gently laid Cade in the bathtub. It was safer than the sink and she wanted both of her hands free to start going through the cupboards.

And the thought of relief for her aching arms and back had also been in there somewhere.

3

"Well Cade, who knew someone could have so much stuff?!"

As expected the cabinets had been well stocked with all sorts of creams and tonics and even a few odd 'devices' like face-steamers – or at least that was what Jessa thought it was. Eventually she found a section with pills, painkillers, and band aids and now Jessa was at the next difficult task of figuring out what she could give Cade.

"I guess there was little chance of it being easy enough that we'd find some 'Baby-Aspirin', hey Cade. No, why would anything ever be simple in this new world?!...what *is* the difference between baby aspirin and regular aspirin anyway? Is it a lower dosage do you think? Could I just, like, give you half or a quarter of a regular aspirin and that would be the same?...although how the hell am I going to get you to take a tablet? You're barely eating now as it is!"

Jessa gently carried Cade back downstairs. "Okay, let's try this. Our neighbours were going on a holiday and they asked us to look after their dog. It was really old and had all these things wrong with it and it was like, on every medication available. Now, because it was a dog of course it didn't want to take tablet and Mum and I had to get 'creative'. We tried hiding it in food, holding him down and stuffing them down his throat – but it always seemed to come back up again but in various stages of digestion. And in the end we used to ground them up into a powder and sprinkle it on his food. He'd lap it all right up and be none the wiser!"

She headed back to the kitchen and after only a little searching, found a mortar and pestle.

"Okay, so we'll take it easy first time round," she said, cutting one of the aspirin tablet first in half and then into quarters. However by the time she finished crushing up the first quarter, even she had to admit there didn't seem to be a whole lot left. Not even really enough for her to try and pinch between her fingers and feed to Cade. So then, after consulting the back of the packet and realizing that an adult dose was two tablets, Jessa crushed up one whole tablet figuring best case scenario she would get maybe half of a tablet into Cade's system.

"That's going to have to be enough kid. The rest is going to be up to you." Jessa consulted the back of the packet again. "Repeat every three to four hours, not exceeding six doses a day," she read aloud. "Okay kid, I'll think about giving you some more in another four to five hours – just in case. In the meantime though, open up."

She propped him on the kitchen bench, alarmed when his eyes rolled around and he didn't seem able to focus. She scraped as much of the powder as she could onto a spoon. "Sorry about this Cade honey – it's probably not going to taste too good but it'll make you feel better."

She propped his head up so she could open his mouth and put the spoon as far back as she dared before tipping the contents down the back of his throat. It was the kind of thing that she probably never would have been able to do if Cade hadn't been so limp and therefore compliant and after a moment's thought, she grabbed a water bottle and tipped two capfuls of that down his throat as well.

The first one went down okay but the second resulted in a coughing fit and he fought against her. He let out a feeble cry and Jessa cringed at how weak it sounded and all the phlegm he seemed to be trying to bring up. She grabbed him before he could choke and put him over her shoulder and pounded him on the back with as much force as she dared. This caused yet another prolonged coughing fit but at the same time, at least now she could hear him also taking breaths, followed by fresh cries that was only a poor imitation of his usual ones.

"It's okay Cade," Jessa tried to soothed him. "It's okay. You're okay. We're...okay."

Chapter Nineteen –

1

Jessa started off in the little girl's room, searching through the drawers for practical clothes while Cade stared at her with his thumb in his mouth, watching her groggily.

"Now I know this isn't going to be ideal but with fashion the way it is nowadays there should be some gender-neutral options here..." Jessa trailed off as she pushed aside fluffy pink dresses, tutus and pretty princess costumes. "...unless of course we have stumbled across the only kid in the country who doesn't own pants."

She picked out a pair of blue flannel pj's with clouds on them. They were going to be big and she had to roll up the sleeves so much Cade looked like a mini-budda with all the extra rolls but she was pretty sure he felt better getting out of his old sweaty clothes and into something fresh and soft. She even swapped over his singlet for a yellow one with daisy's sewn in the front which actually didn't look so bad.

"I probably should have given you a quick sponge down first but we don't really have time for that, sorry kid."

She searched through the drawers again, this time re-emerging with a purple pair of pjs decorated with ice creams and rainbows and three more singlets. Then it was back to the Master bedroom where she propped Cade in an oversized armchair that was probably less used for sitting as to try and fill up some of the empty space in the room and make it seem less cavernous. Cade went easily enough and Jessa would have worried he was returning back to his catatonic state except he was watching her every move, his eyes following her wherever she went.

"You're probably just feeling mellow now you're in fresh clothes," Jessa said. "A bit like that pleased-with-himself caterpillar in Alice In Wonderland?...or was it the Cheshire Cat?...probably doesn't matter. I'll read the book to you one day though. It's a good story – kind of weird but good for the imagination."

She looked into the closest and the potential avalanche of clothes with trepidation, seeing mostly only women's power-suits and sequined tops and dresses.

"Not exactly practical, eh Cade? But hey, you're in little girl clothes so why can't I wear guy clothes, huh? I'm sure that's what some budget-savvy chicks do anyway." She swapped over her old jeans – that while being practical and durable, has also become quite rank – for a pair of soft track-suit pants. They were so soft and comfortable against her skin that, even though there previously would have been nothing in the world that would have made her wear the two together, Jessa began rummaging around for a matching jacket.

She swapped her current shirt for one of the guy's thermal singlets and what looked like a polo shirt but was made from some kind of green flannel. Truthfully it was actually quite hideous and potentially someone's idea of a 'gag-gift', but it was also warm as all hell and with her own jacket over the top, somewhat hidden.

"There you go Cade," she said. "I guess my standards have seriously dropped but..."

Jessa trailed off when she saw the expression on Cade's face. It was difficult to tell on the face of a toddler but it seemed like at that point he wouldn't have cared if she picked him up and they left or if she went on her own and just left him there. Either way, he was spent.

"Or I'm just projecting," Jessa mumbled, feeling deeply uncomfortable. It wasn't like she hadn't had this thought before but whereas previously it had come from a place of frustration or fear, this time she just felt numb as she imagined picking up her freshly packed bag, walking out of the room, down the stairs and out the front door. And the thing about the look on Cade's face was that he would watch her do it as simply as he had been watching her go through the drawers.

He wouldn't complain or cry or wail for her to come back this time. He wouldn't roll himself off the chair and try to follow her crawling or tottering on his unsteady legs. He would just continue to lay there, sucking his thumb quietly until someone – or some*thing* – else showed up or he closed his eyes and slipped away.

"Okay Cade," she said, trying to shake this off, her face reddening with shame. "Let's try to come up with a plan here."

And that was when there was a loud thump above them.

Chapter Twenty –

1

'I had to leave him downstairs,' Jessa repeated. 'I *had* to...it's safer! That way if there is something upstairs and we have to get out quick I can just bolt down the stairs and grab him.'

Of course all of this did nothing to combat her anxiety at letting him out of her sight even for a few minutes. Even this felt akin to abandonment and coming close to what had dangerously been the real thing only a few minutes ago.

She could have just left the house and taken their chances with the night – except like it or not, Cade couldn't spend another night outside and she *needed* to start acting like a responsible adult. And this was the only shelter around and she was more than ready to put her feet up.

So she slowly climbed the stairs, getting to the second floor and peering around the corner into a hallway that had seemed perfectly safe and fine a little while ago but which now felt like a gauntlet of danger and possible death.

'And here I thought I had moved on from all the dramatic stuff,' she thought. She could even see the chain dangling from the roof that would pull the ladder down to get to the attic, seemingly as neutral as before.

However, feeling like a horror movie cliché, Jessa slowly reached for the chain.

2

Jessa she couldn't explain why this was bothering her so much – especially considering all the other horrors she had seen. In fact, compared to some of them, this was almost tame!

Jessa had grabbed a poker from one of the fireplaces and at the top of the ladder spotted a torch and decided to view this as a positive sign. It meant that at some point there had been people up here but positioned where it was now, likely meant they were gone now.

'...so what the hell is making the noises?'

It hadn't taken her that long to spot the culprit considering the attic space hadn't been used as a storage and so it was mostly empty. A dead woman chained up to the far wall with what looked suspiciously like bike chains and bungee cords.

"What the fuck?" Jessa had muttered and had been standing there, confused ever since.

The woman was dressed in a pink, satin dressing gown, a cream lacy romper underneath. Completely inappropriate for the current seasonal temperature Jessa thought but then again, the creature probably didn't care anymore. It was of course now dirty, stained with blood and something darker, as was the woman's chin which Jessa began to see more of as it snapped and pulled at the restraints, reacting to her presence.

The smell was especially ripe and at first Jessa thought it was all coming from the woman, except there was also the scent of fresh blood and as Jessa shone the flashlight around, she saw the bodies of several small animals tossed in a plastic tub in the far corner of the room. None of them whole anymore, looking like they had been torn apart and the leftovers tossed in the tub. Some of the bodies were older than others and as Jessa glanced back to the woman she realized the situation.

"Someone's been feeding you," she muttered and it was this image that made her stomach do even crazier and more extreme leaps than it already had been.

She shone the flashlight a little further, not having to go far to find a single air mattress set up in the opposite corner between the dead woman and her 'meals'. There were a few blankets, a pillow and a small, battery powered nightlight that probably played a tune and danced stars across the roof when it was dark and whoever this person was, needed comfort. It seemed like the kind of thing a four year old would have treasured and thus, went completely against the books stacked up next to the 'bed' – 'An introduction to Shakespeare', 'The Canterbury

Tales' by Chaucer, and 'The Big Book of Facts and Experiments for Boys'.

She turned back to the dead woman, assuming she had been the original owner of all the clothes and make-up and well, *stuff* from downstairs. "If only you could see yourself now," Jessa murmured, taking a very, very cautious step closer, not sure how much to trust the restraints.

The dead lady probably had an expertly done blonde dye-job but the darkness of the attic made it hard to tell. Her skin wasn't just pale but a grey colour that would have been the sign of coming rain if seen in the sky. It hung off in places, sagging from her bones as though she was losing what little muscle definition she had and eventually all that would be left would be bones. Her eyes had sunken in, the pupils turning white and the white part, bloodshot. Her original eye colour should have been indistinguishable except one of her iris's was still a bright, vibrant blue that had Jessa confused. Her teeth were bloodstained and as Jessa moved a tiny bit closer and saw that the various ties had positioned the woman to one of the support beams of the roof and actually did look secure. The woman didn't just have the stench of blood and the dead animals she had been fed but the smell indicating she must have lost control of her bowels in the last few moments before she had turned or mutated or died – whatever it was that happened.

Her clothes had a few tears in them – mostly at the neck and the shoulder where it looked like someone had grabbed her and used her dressing gown to man-handle her. And when Jessa took a careful step around her to look at the back of her head, she saw it was flattened and crushed in, small bits of skulls still caught up in the woman's hair and oozing down her back until it had dried into a lumpy mess.

'Okay so someone – maybe a family friend or a neighbour – ran into the house...or caught 'Mother' here outside getting the paper first thing in the morning considering there wasn't any mess anywhere in the house and this sure as hell must have created a whole bunch of damage – did their thing, and then moved on. Then 'Kid' either woke up or came home from a sleepover or from just being somewhere safe which meant they hadn't been killed too. They discovered Mummy, dragged her upstairs before she had woken up and started to attack, tied her up and has been trying to do their best to care for her ever since. Feeding her, maybe even reading to her, sleeping up here with her – and hoping she would get better or someone would show up to help.'

Of course there were several flaws with this interpretation.

'Hell, maybe it's not even a kid at all but some kind of Antony Perkins-Psycho who thinks this woman is his mother...or has one of those mental deficits where he's the size of a house but has the mental capacity of a grade-schooler hence how he got her up here...but why he has been reading *those* books. It would probably be best to get the hell out of here before he comes back with some fresh meals for her – maybe as presents for *mother*.'

All of these thoughts raced through Jessa's mind and it all seemed perfectly logical and yet still she hesitated. For some reason it bothered her that one of the woman's eyes was still such a perfect blue. Maybe it was important or a clue on how to ultimately 'fix' them.

The blue was just so bright and unnatural and the other one, almost white. Maybe she only went crazy when the sun went down like a werewolf. Or maybe it was a 'stages' thing and this was the next one after going crazy. Or maybe –

"Hey! – what are you doing here?!" a voice asked from behind her.

3

Jessa felt a little faint, she was *that* scared. She stayed where she was, frozen in place, staring at the dead thing in front of her and wondering how long it was going to be before she joined its ranks.

'You idiot! You total idiot! You've walked right into this trap and –
'

"I said, what are you doing here?! You can't be here! – you better get out right now! What are you doing to her – leave her alone!"

The more the person spoke, the longer Jessa felt better because she recognized the tone.

It was a little girl.

Chapter Twenty-One –

1

"I'm not going to hurt you," Jessa said. Moving as slowly as she dared – which was truthfully *very* slow because she was still feeling a little light-headed from her fright, she turned to face the girl. "I just heard a noise and wanted to see what it was...could you please move the light out of my eyes?"

Jessa had paused when she was still side on, her face slightly turned away with the torch she had hijacked now pointed at the ceiling. But the girl had another one – a much *brighter* one it seemed – and was pointing it directly at her face.

"How did you get in here?!" the girl demanded, not lowering her torch an inch.

"I pulled the chain down from the roof – "

"I mean my house!" the girl said angrily, causing the light to bob up slightly.

"Well...I didn't think anyone lived here and I needed help with my...it...is there anyone else with you?" she asked, thinking there was no way a little girl could have survived on her own and hoped she hadn't made a major mistake by leaving Cade downstairs, unprotected and –

But she didn't get any further with her thought as the dead woman behind her suddenly lunged not at Jessa who was by far closer but towards the little girl – or more specifically, what she had in her hand.

Jessa couldn't see it for herself – the little girl was little more than a vague silhouette – but she still reacted instinctively, dropping to the floor and rolling at the same time, stopping only when she reached a far wall and bounced back.

At the exact same time the little girl yelled out, "Mum, no!" reaching out for her with the hand that held a dead animal. In her haste to get it to the snapping dead thing the girl over-estimated the distance and in Jessa's opinion got *far* too close. And, unable to stop herself Jessa raced over, lifting the girl completely off the floor and holding her back.

"Hey, put me down!"

"Watch it! You've got to be careful of these things!"

"You think I don't know that?! One of these *things* did this to my mother!" The girl kicked out with her legs, catching Jessa in her shins so she cursed and dropped her. Moving with impressive speed, the girl ducked out of her arms and across the room, still clutching whatever animal she had caught for her mother's supper.

"Please, I don't mean to hurt you," Jessa said. "In fact, I'll even leave if you would just move away from the ladder..."

The girl just stared though. "What were you doing with her?" she demanded.

"I was looking at her eyes," Jessa said. "I haven't seen any of the dead ones with eyes like that."

"What'd you mean, dead ones?" the girl said sharply and Jessa realized this girl was apparently working under the assumption her mother was just acting temporarily homicidal and would eventually go back to normal.

"Um...that's just what I call them...I don't really know what they are or what's wrong with them...anyway, none of the others have eyes like that."

"They're contacts," the girl said. "Before she...got angry...she said they were bothering her. I only got one of them out and she hasn't let me get close enough to get the other."

"But the colour..."

"Mum wears coloured ones. She says they make her eyes 'pop'...or whatever." There was something in the girl's voice and the way she described it that made Jessa know this was usually accompanied by an eyeroll.

"How did you get her up here?"

"Dad did it. He went out and – he should be coming back any minute though!" she added in a rush.

"How long ago?"

"Long enough to be here soon. He went for food so don't bother thinking we have anything for you to take!"

Jessa again glanced down at the dead animal in the girl's hand, willing to keep the light away from it because she didn't want to know exactly what animal she was serving up tonight. "Don't worry. We don't want any of your stuff."

The girl's hands suddenly balled into fists and Jessa thought she saw a fine tremble go through her body. "We?!" the girl asked. "Who is *we*?!"

'Well, at least I know she didn't find Cade,' Jessa thought – and then had her slower reflexes further emphasized when the girl suddenly threw the animal at her and bolted down the ladder.

Jessa instinctively flinched away from the dead creature, feeling a soft thud as it hit her body and then instant skin-crawling sensation of knowing it was dead. Jessa had no idea why this bothered her so much considering one such dead thing was now straining against her ties to reach the other on the floor.

"So I guess your mother can fend for herself, then?" Jessa yelled on impulse. She felt cruel but it was enough to cause the girl to hesitate with the top of her head poking up. The girl started to visibly shake, tears shining on her face and her lower lip trembling as she looked up at her with pleading.

"Please don't hurt her," she said quietly. "Or me. Please – it's already – so hard – " She did one of those hiccup sobs and Jessa realized the girl was dangerously close to losing her grip on the ladder and she rushed to grab her hand before she could fall.

2

Jessa sat across from Hailey on one of the matching couches with Cade beside her, trying to follow her story. However Hailey hadn't talked to someone in so long and was talking so fast – and Jessa's focus was split anyway, wondering if that noise was the little girl's mother managing to get her hands on the dead cat and was munching on it or if she had broken free and sensing there was something so much more tastier down the ladder and so –

"And so he left...I don't know – about a week ago, maybe? It's getting harder to keep track. I didn't realize how much Mum used to remind me of this stuff. I keep waiting for him to come home – he wouldn't have gone this long without something happening to him. Before all of this he wouldn't even let me go outside half the time – even when I was with him! But I had to go out a lot on my own to look for food and...stuff...for Mum. She's lost it. I mean, she was always did weird stuff but she got even weirder after everyone else started getting angry. And then she went outside and got hurt by Mr Francas from down the road. That was really weird too because he used to be this really old man who couldn't move very well and Mum did those spin-cycle classes – or whatever they're called – for *years*, so she's always been super-fit."

"Anyway, Mum said – Dad and me weren't there because we'd gone around to check on Grandma Pat and she wasn't home when we got there either, just a whole bunch of glass because someone tore through the place. Dad got really sad...but anyway Mum said she was walking out to check the mail and Mr Francas came up and chased her around the house and caught her and tried to bite her and all kinds of bad stuff. Mum killed him using this spear that Dad has for the garden when he needed to make a big hole in the ground. Dad wouldn't let me look at Mr Francas but I've seen what it could do when Dad first bought it, so it was probably pretty gross. You know, to get used on a person."

"Dad burned him later that day. And then Mum started to get sick. She got a fever and stopped talking and then she started hitting herself and then trying to hit us. Dad tied her up and put her in the attic, saying we had to keep her i-so-late-ed until the police or the army or whatever, came and helped us..." Hailey looked down at the floor as though she knew it wasn't right but then added defiantly, "She has to eat doesn't she? We learnt that in school and it always says so in books when they talk about us not having anorexia or bulimia or whatever."

Jessa held her hands up. "To each their own. I just hope you were being careful, that's all."

Hailey nodded. "I am – I wear oven mitts! Which makes it really hard when I have to hold things 'cause, you know, oven mitts. I didn't let myself take them off though and then she was growling at me so I brought her some of our regular food and she wouldn't eat it and..." She stole another glance at Jessa and then went back to the floor. "...I had a ham sandwich – Dad said it was still okay to eat because it'd been frozen – and she seemed to like that...she ate it all anyway. So I began to get this idea that maybe she needed meat – the opposite of what she usually eats because she's always been about salads and vegetables and stuff – and she's normally so careful about how she looks so I thought that maybe whatever this thing is – virus or whatever – makes people the opposite of what they usually are...anyway..." Hailey tapered off and didn't seem to know how to finish.

"And then I came along," Jessa summed up for her and realized she only had one question left. "Um...what's with the books?"

Hailey shrugged again. "It's boring here on my own with no TV."

"I get that, but Chaucer? Isn't that a little old and...*weird* for a kid?"

"Yeah, I don't get most of it and the words are really long. But it's...it's kind of like a song...and it...soothes her, maybe? She listens anyway and sometimes she even stops thrashing."

Jessa thought more likely the mother was tiring herself out and taking a rest. Then again dead people weren't supposed to get tired so what the hell did she know.

"Where are you going to?" Hailey asked, watching her.

"Home," Jessa replied simply.

"What direction? Did you pass the big shopping centre on the main road? You can tell it because the sign is the shape of a big cowboy hat that dances when it's dark. It's because there's a restaurant on the same turn that plays cowboy music and serves steak and BBQ. That was where my Dad was going because he said the shopping centre might have food left on the shelves."

Jessa couldn't remember so shook her head. She didn't hold out much hope for the girl's father since she doubted a parent would have left their child alone for this long unless something had gone wrong.

"You know, you can stay if you want," Hailey said so quietly Jessa barely heard her.

"That's nice of you to offer. It would only be for one night. I've got to get home to my own mother and then...I don't know actually."

"You want your mother," Hailey said. "Yeah, I get that."

3

Jessa should have known it had to a dire situation for Hailey's Dad to leave his daughter alone to venture out for food.

"It's the same with all the neighbours," Hailey said as Jessa stared at the empty pantry. She then resumed trying to play a game with Cade who didn't seem all that interested but did occasionally push the ball back which Jessa was taking as a good sign.

"What about the next street over?"

Hailey shrugged. "Not sure. I don't think Dad wanted to go to them though. He said it would be break 'n' entering and when everything went back to normal he didn't want to explain to them about why we thought we could just help ourselves."

'Sounds promising,' Jessa thought and suggested Hailey stay here with Cade while Jessa went out in search of dinner.

"But I should come with you – you don't know my neighbours, they might, like, attack you or something if you go into their house!" Hailey said, matching every step Jessa took towards the backdoor.

"I'll knock before I enter and if I come across anybody, I'll get the hell out. The thing is, I can't take Cade with me – he's sick and he should be inside as much as possible. And because he's a baby, I – *we* – can't leave him alone. I need you to stay with him. Besides, I'm just going next door."

Of course the house 'next-door' was actually going to be quite a hike but Jessa was out of options.

"You'll be fine Hailey – you will," Jessa said, putting a hand on the girl's shoulder. "I'm not going far. I just *really* need you to look after Cade."

"And what if – or when – *you* don't come back?" she asked, panic clear on her face. "What do I do then?"

"Then I guess...you just have to keep doing your best." This sounded lame even to Jessa and Hailey's father had probably said something similar when he left. But it was a better answer then her first impulse which was to beg, "Well then please don't feed Cade to your mother."

Chapter Twenty-Two –

1

Throughout this whole ordeal Jessa had never felt more like she was in the middle of a horror movie than she did right now. 'And rather than staying inside the warm, safe house, I have done the victim thing of wandering outside to have a look. Great.'

She stuffed her hands in her pockets, her breathed puffing out in front of her face. There weren't many things to hide behind out here if she needed it. 'Not even a bush to fall asleep under if I suddenly get the overwhelming urge to nap again,' she thought mocking herself.

She walked straight across the lawn and then for a childish reason she didn't totally understand, veered off towards the garden beds, stomping all over the flowers. It was a frenzy of behaviour that didn't feel good or release her pent up frustration but more just that pretty flowers and neat flowerbeds didn't belong in this world anymore. Maybe it would in the future but at this particular moment, it was out of place and wrong.

Or maybe she was just throwing a temper tantrum.

Jessa stopped at the first house she came to – it *looked* empty enough so she went around to the back door. She kicked in the glass pane near the door handle, letting herself into a small hall that she figured was what was called a butler's pantry. Then through a laundry area and finally the kitchen – and straight into a mess, her feet crunching on a carpet of cereal.

"What the hell?" she muttered. It was like someone had knocked over a box at some point and not bothered to clean it up. The rest of the cupboards looked equally ran-sacked but she still checked.

She automatically avoided the fridge, skidding slightly over the muck on the floor to get to the cupboards. Some were completely empty, others full of cleaning products, and then finally she found something of use. "Tuna," she read on one of the label. Could babies be fed *fish*?

There was a tin of sweet corn as well, one of peaches in juice and then some cat food which Jessa put beside the tuna but then thought about the implications of *that* and with purpose, tossed it over her shoulder to add to the mess already on the floor. It made a low thud and a strange kind of rustling which she assumed was the can rolling and otherwise paid no attention to as she crouched to check the lowest shelves, not wanting to miss anything.

Then a male voice from behind her spoke. "Stop right where you are pretty thang."

3

Jessa waited to feel afraid again like when Hailey had snuck up on her but if anything she felt disengaged. Like she was watching a movie or television or something. She obeyed the voice and thought only how she hoped he wouldn't keep her like this for long because her thighs were going to cramp up.

"What are you doing here?" he asked.

"Looking for food. I thought this place was empty but it's not so I'll just leave – "

"I said don't move!"

Jessa wasn't close enough to the door yet so she stayed where she was, her hands half-raised to show she didn't have anything in them and waited.

"Turn around."

Jessa did so, also wanting to scrutinize the man holding her hostage. He looked about thirty, shoulder-length, greasy blonde hair under a beanie, almost a week's worth of stubble, grubby clothes and holding what looked very much like a BB gun pointed at her mid-section.

It wasn't the gun though that was making all her never-endings tingle and twitch. There was just something about the guy that felt...off.

"Who are you?" he asked.

"That doesn't matter."

"It doesn't?" he said with a raised eyebrow.

"Once you let me walk out that door, you'll never see me again."

"And I'm just supposed to believe you?"

"If I had known someone else had claimed this place then I would have kept moving. I don't want any trouble and I don't think you do either...isn't there enough dead people around without the two of us starting something?"

He suddenly smiled at her, as though he couldn't help it. "Sorry," he said. "I didn't mean to be this way. It's just...people – even the still okay ones – are...different...these days."

"Yeah, I've noticed that too. But like I said – if you let me leave now then you'll never see me again and – "

"Wait! Are you alone?"

Jessa hesitated.

"Not that I mean anything by it," he added. "I just...I'm on my own and I've met a lot of people who were on their own to – I mean there were a couple that were together but usually...so what I'm saying is it can get kind of...lonely."

Jessa leant back on the cabinets, possibly looking like she was relaxing but really she wanted to be in a good position to get her legs up and kick him away if he suddenly decided to pounce on her. "So why didn't you stay with the couple if you want to be around people?"

"Just 'cause *I* want to be around people doesn't mean they want to be around me. Plus – it's not exactly safe out there anymore!"

"It's not exactly safe in here either," Jessa said, indicating his gun with a nod of her head.

He lowered his weapon and set it down next to the cupboard – but still within reaching distance Jessa noted. "I thought you might want some company as much as me...you're welcome to leave if you really want to. But you might want to reconsider since..." He motioned over her shoulder.

Jessa glanced over her shoulder quickly at first, then stopping to take a much longer look. "Shit."

3

"What do you think is attracting them?" Jessa asked in a hushed voice.

"Who knows? Maybe they're heading for the city."

"Why?"

"That's where people are?" he suggested. "I mean, they keep saying on the radio how there are rescue centres and that people should go there if they want help."

"Are they for real?"

"What'd you mean?"

"Are they *real* safe-havens?"

"I guess so. It just doesn't seem to me to be a good idea to gather in big groups because it draws them."

Jessa felt a shiver at the implications of this – the human race permanently 'scattered' to avoid detection.

So far the group of about thirty or so dead outside had left them alone – Jessa had ducked down behind the cupboards the minute she saw them and the guy had followed suit, both of them crouching low, Jessa waiting for the inevitable sound of breaking glass as the dead attacked.

For several minutes there was nothing but the sounds of those outside moving and shuffling and letting out the occasional growl.

"How long is this going to last for?" she asked in a whisper to the guy. With some silent motions and arm movements they had agreed to move into the living room where the curtains were closed, providing more coverage but where they could still track the movements outside thanks to the shadows cast by the moon.

"I've only ever come across one group the size of this one and they were gone after about an hour."

"Where'd they go?"

"I told you – towards the city. Beyond that I don't know because I opted to go in the *other* direction as fast as I could. What about you?"

"I ran into one other crowd but they were all whipped up into a frenzy because they had stumbled across survivors. We got away in the melee."

Jessa was so strung out she didn't realize she had used the expression "we" until she noticed the interest in the guy's face and then decided there was no point in pretending. "I had a kid with me at the time and I think I'm going to end up responsible for another I met only a couple of hours ago."

"Where are they now?"

'Hopefully safe,' Jessa thought, trying to reassure herself by imagining Cade and Hailey playing in the lounge room, Hailey looking up and seeing the zombie parade and grabbing Cade to hide back up in the attic again. To the guy though, Jessa just waved her hand in a random direction. "I had to leave them somewhere safe while I went to look for food."

"So you don't have any food then?" A strange glint in his eye.

"We're okay. But I wanted a few more tins in case food becomes a little scarcer on the road and we run out."

"Where are you going?"

"Home. We've still got a distance to go."

"And how are you getting there?'

"On foot mostly. A car just seemed more trouble than it was worth."

"I've got a car."

"Good for you," Jessa said tiredly.

"I mean, I could probably give you a lift – if you need."

"Oh yeah? And why would you do that?"

He shrugged and then looked at her carefully. Jessa didn't notice because she had gone back to staring out the window, relieved the trek of dead appeared to be thinning.

"So...how old are they? The kids, I mean."

"Why?"

"I was...just wondering if they're really safe to be on their own."

Jessa shrugged. "Cade is a baby, about one – one and a half maybe. Hailey is older."

"How much...older?"

"Not a teenager yet."

"That's nice. You know...you could probably get wherever you want faster if you had a car...and maybe we could work something out."

"Something out?" Jessa repeated.

"No I was more thinking I could drop you home as a trade. Maybe even share a few cans of food I've managed to scrounge up from nearby houses..."

"And what, all I have to do is give a little demonstration of just how grateful I am?"

If the guy noticed the acid in her tone he didn't react to it, instead staring at her avidly, his tongue half-way out of his mouth as though he was going to lick his lips only he had become too preoccupied by his own fantasies.

"Well...not *you*."

4

Jessa felt like her soul had been shoved in the freezer and she was never going to thaw again. She tried to figure out a way she might have misheard him. That way all she needed to do was smile, roll her eyes and move on, pretending people as vile as this didn't exist anymore. However her jaw felt locked in place and the moment endless as she stared at him.

"...all I'd really want is thirty minutes alone...not that bad considering what I'm offering you..."

Jessa must have hesitated for too long though or maybe he noticed the stiffness in her body because his own eyes narrowed and he suddenly threw himself at her.

His weapon seemingly forgotten, he landed with his full body weight almost crushing her except Jessa had positioned herself against a sideboard near the window. It now gave her something extra to brace against so rather than landing with him on top, she was temporarily trapped between the two opposing forces, feeling the air knocked out of her but otherwise not hurt.

"Where are they? Just tell me, huh. Tell me where they are and I'll take *real* good care of 'em."

He tried to punch but his centre of gravity was off and he couldn't put any power behind his hits. Jessa couldn't breathe but overall she was surprisingly calm as she told herself he would tire out and then she would have the advantage. He was practically sitting in her lap with his face so close she could have reached out and kissed him – or bitten off his nose which was her *true* impulse – but something else had taken over, soothing her and simultaneously leaving her cold and calculating.

Jessa just needed to pick her moment, then reach up and poke him in the eye.

Unfortunately in the same way *he* hadn't been able to get leverage, Jessa also couldn't put quite as much force she wanted to because of her cramped position. However, with a spot like the eye, Jessa discovered she didn't need much.

Her finger pushed against his eye socket easily and while he was able to jerk back so she didn't puncture his eyeball like she wanted, he did fall away and Jessa now leapt on top of him. She reached for the knife tucked in her belt but he blocked her wrist in time and pushed her away quite easily, making her fully aware of just how much stronger he was. She fell against the sideboard for a second time, jarring her arm but rounding back on him and preparing to duck since she felt sure he was going to throw a punch again. However he lashed out with his foot instead, catching her off guard as he drove it into her knee and then a fist into her stomach when she instinctively doubled over to protect her limb.

This pain was so incredible she crumpled to the floor, wondering if he had managed to shove all of her internal organs out of place, hence explaining the strange lump at the back of her throat.

His next kick was aimed at her face but she threw herself to the side at the last minute, watching his foot sail past her and into the wall, creating a small dent. The guy was thrown off balance by his miss and Jessa now grabbed this foot, pushing to get him to the ground while at the same time using it as leverage to pull herself to her feet. It didn't quite work as well as she would have liked as he fell against the couch, the cramped space they were attempting to fight inside working just as much in his favour as hers.

He kicked at her again but Jessa sat on a side table slightly so that she was now able to use her legs to kick him, aiming for his groin with everything she had. He let out a kind of sound Jessa had never heard from another human being, clutching and cuddling over his body as though he could now protect himself from something that had already happened. Her hand convulsed around the knife she had forgotten she was holding and she suddenly lunged forward with it, aiming for the side of his neck.

The knife slid in so easily that for a second Jessa thought she'd missed. But when she tried to pull back to try again she felt the resistance.

The shadows and darkness of the night took most of the colour away and Jessa was only faintly aware of the dark puddle spreading out from underneath his body and how his throat had become so covered it looked like he was wearing a scarf.

The knife in her hand was slick with blood and her jacket too was covered. She dropped the knife and quickly shrugged off the jacket, leaving it to pool on the floor.

'Doesn't matter,' she thought. 'Hailey's mother had plenty of them in her wardrobe. I'll just replace it.'

5

Jessa regretted dropping her coat far sooner. The cold *had* to be the reason why she was shivering. It had nothing to do with what she had just done and how she now felt like screaming or running out into the dead ones and seeing if they would turn around and attack her or just accept her as one of their own – just another crazed, sadistic killer joining their ranks.

All the strength in her legs run out at once and she fell to the floor with a thump and such force it should have hurt but Jessa didn't feel it.

'What if he comes back as one of those crazy-ones?' she wondered idly. She wanted to curl into a little ball and hide until everything was better again – or at least, until enough time had passed and enough layers had formed over the memory that she could pretend it had been a dream. The last time this happened – with Sheryl – Cade had been there to remind her that giving up wasn't an option. This time however, he was far away, her recollection of him, fuzzy and dreamy. And easy to dismiss.

Jessa had ended up cross-legged on the entry rug with her arms around herself. She wasn't rocking as a source of comfort yet but was considering it. She was also crying, slow and silent. The kind of crying a person did when they were at a funeral and past the point of being anything but raw emotion.

And what was she mourning? Herself, maybe. For the 'good' person she used to be and who hadn't been capable of such things and the lengths they would go to survive – not just for themselves, but for someone they loved.

Jessa froze in her thoughts.

"I really do love that damn kid," she whispered.

It was a revelation because she had thought she was looking after him out of a sense of duty – similar to how she would have been forced to care for a puppy abandoned on the side of the road before taking it to an animal shelter or something. She had never considered herself anything more than a glorified, temporary baby-sitter.

Now though, it finally occurred to her that she did feel something for the kid. She wasn't just his care-taker and she couldn't just pass him along and forget about him as soon as someone more responsible came along. And she couldn't just leave him to survive on his own.

"Damn," she muttered and was surprised when her voice came out loud and clear.

She slowly stood up, her legs so wobbly she had to brace herself against the wall, her head also spinning strangely, making the world off-kilter.

"Stop thinking so much," she advised herself. "That's what's causing the trouble. The future doesn't exist yet and it's just this one moment now."

She let that thought ferment for a while, deciding that the pressure she felt on her shoulders was purely her imagination, *not* the actual weight of a dead body settling –

"Shake it off Jess!" Her vision narrowed to a point and she took two steps before dropping back beside the guy. Thankfully she only had to go as high as his jacket pockets to find his car keys but by the time she was done her fingers were sticky with blood and she left a small trail of fingerprints as she crawled into the kitchen. She was still wary of the parade of dead – although now that she thought about it, she hadn't seen anything move by the windows lately.

'He might have been lying about the car though...or he might have hidden it...or it might be a total piece of shit that won't even start...or...'

She didn't find it in the garage but parked outside not far from where she had first come in. A little, two-door mini that had probably been a teenage girl's first car judging by the flower-sticker window decals and dream catcher hanging from the mirror. It was clean enough inside and Jessa was grateful to see that the automatic lock had been disabled because it meant she didn't have to worry about lights flashing when she unlocked it. The dead crowd seemed have moved on but that didn't mean they couldn't come back.

Jessa glanced in the back seat and discovered three guns, a baseball bat, what looked like a hockey-stick and maybe even an axe hiding under the seat on the floor. But more importantly there was a crate of bottled water behind the other seat and what looked like two or three plastic bags of food.

Jessa glanced once more at the house, wondering if there was anything else she needed to do.

"It won't matter if there is," she repeated out loud, locking the car door and then promptly resting her head on the steering wheel, hysterically sobbing. "I want my mother."

Chapter Twenty-Three –

1

"Are you absolutely sure you won't come with us?" Jessa asked Hailey. She had spent two days with the girl, Hailey not exactly flourishing under having someone to look after her but seemingly enjoying the company.

Jessa hadn't returned that first night until almost day break. She wasn't entirely sure where the rest of the hours had gone but strongly suspected she might have cried herself to sleep in the car or at least had hysterics bad enough to black out for a few hours. Either way she had awoken with a jerk and in the midst of a nightmare of the man rising from the dead and just about to break through the glass of the window of the car and kill her.

The dream had been so vivid that when Jessa had woken up, she had slammed back against the head-rest and then forward on the steering wheel, causing the horn to let out a short toot but loud enough to make Jessa feel like her heart stop for almost half a minute, her vision going grey around the edges. She had then slumped over in the seat, faint as her body reacted to her extreme fear.

She had wanted to throw herself into the dark space in front of the passenger seat, scrunch up and stay like that until she felt safe again – which she slowly realized was probably going to be never.

So instead she had blown her clogged up nose on the bottom of her shirt – 'I'll just grab another one from Hailey's Mum too,' – and then wondered how successful she was going to be, driving without any streetlights to guide her.

She drove past Hailey's house twice, back-tracking when she realized she was almost on the highway and then again when she had ended up back where she had started.

Hailey had naturally been very pleased to see her – and even Cade had come waddling forward. She had shared the food around, refusing to offer much explanation of where it had come from and how she had gotten the car.

"It's not important. It's ours now."

Jessa had then headed upstairs and immediately fallen asleep after making sure the car was hidden in the garage and giving Hailey a vague warning about keeping an eyes out for a mob of dead ones.

She had woken up around the mid-afternoon, sure she'd heard screaming downstairs and bolting to check, only to find Hailey playing with Cade quietly and the two of them looking at her with confusion when she burst in. Jessa had sat on the couch wordlessly for almost two hours, feeling icy cold despite the blankets and layers she wrapped around herself.

Then when the two kids had gone to sleep and Jessa had taken up watch in the front room, she had begun to go over in her head exactly what she was meant to do *now*.

She wasn't staying here but could she really leave Hailey on her own to survive like this? What would have happened to her if that guy had found her before Jessa? The girl wouldn't leave her mother so was she supposed to force her into her car, effectively kidnapping her. What was to stop her from leaping out at the first opportunity? Jessa could be harsh, go upstairs and kill the mother thus freeing Hailey from whatever responsibility she was feeling but would she forgive Jessa afterwards? And who was *Jessa* to think she knew what was best?

She had checked on a sleeping Hailey, Cade in the same bed (and apparently doing the same thing he always did – hog the blankets) and then crept past them, upstairs to the decaying woman. It had mostly snarled at her, leaving Jessa little doubt there was no one home but then something strange happened.

Jessa started to see the face of her own mother over this woman's who had probably cared for her own daughter just as much and who was now nothing more than a monster who would have happily ripped Hailey's throat out.

Jessa had fled from the attic, out of breath and barely able to keep from passing out.

So all she was left with, was leaving Hailey with detailed directions.

"You sure you've got it?" Jessa asked yet again.

"Sure," she mumbled. "You've said it to me five times – enough to make me memorize it. And you've also written it down in that weird code no one else is going to understand but you and me."

"So if your father comes back – "

"When."

"...when. Tell him where all the extra food came from and then where we went so he can follow...or come see us...or whatever – if he wants to. 'Kay?"

"Sure."

"And...in case he *doesn't* come back...or maybe if you get a bit...lonely, you can always come visit. Maybe stay for a couple of days."

"I couldn't leave Mum. Who would feed her if I wasn't around? – I wouldn't want her to starve." Her eyes shifted to the side slightly when she talked about her mother starving, enough to make Jessa wonder if the girl was starting to realize the truth – but apparently not enough to abandon the dead woman completely just yet.

"Okay, well that's it then – "

"You could always come back and visit me too," Hailey said suddenly. "You can find *your* way back..."

"Sure," Jessa said, wondering what could possibly cause her to do something as foolish as venture back out into this violent nightmare of a world. "It might be a while though – especially if something happens to the car...but maybe you could come with us and we could leave a note for your Dad about where we're going! I would take the risk of not having it in code and..."

"But we'd have to put Mum in the backseat with Cade and that probably wouldn't be too safe."

'Agreed,' Jessa thought, shuddering at the suggestion.

"I'll be fine," Hailey said, trying to be brave but ruining the image by having a slight trembling to her bottom lip. "I was doing okay before you came. And Dad's gotta be back soon."

"Sure he will," Jessa said. "Just remember what I said, okay? Stay away from the cities because that seems to be where a lot of the...crazies...are. Don't trust anyone you don't know them – not even women or other kids because they might *still* be dangerous."

"I get it...are you sure you can't stay just one more night?" Hailey mumbled, watching the wind playing with a rusting garden pinwheel as though *that* was important. "After all it's probably safer for you to travel at night anyway. At least that's what my Dad thought which is why he would only go out looking for stuff at night."

"He's probably right but I don't trust myself to drive when it's dark and still know where I'm going...so...I'm sure I'm going to see you and your Dad again and then – " Hailey suddenly threw herself at Jessa, hugging her fiercely. Jessa held her back just as tightly, trying to project what little power or strength – or even luck if that was what it was – that had kept her surviving with Cade, onto Hailey too.

"Oh Hailey," she started to say and then the girl was gone, running for the house and disappearing around the side almost in the blink of an eye.

"Am I doing the right thing?' she asked Cade, but he was exploring the backseat of the car, oblivious to anything else.

2

"She's going to love you, you know," Jessa said, shifting Cade to her other hip. The car had died about two kilometres back, simply running out of petrol and rolling to a stop. The low warning light had been flashing for quite some time but the closest petrol station would have involved driving not just completely out of her way, but closer to the city.

Still, she had been lulled by how long it had been flashing at her that she had begun to fantasize about it being a flaw in the consul or a crossed wire or something.

But then the car had begun to chug and then, nothing.

"At least we have to be thankful it stopped on a flat piece of road, right kid?" Jessa said, huffing slightly and surprised by how quickly she had forgotten the weight of lugging around the kid. "If we had been on a hill then we would have rolled backwards all the way."

She wasn't entirely sure that was right – after all, the parking brake still worked – but she was trying to distract herself because she was starting to recognize parts of her surroundings.

That tree which had somehow survived each and every storm and which still had the scar in it's trunk from where that kid had gone straight into it on his bike, not only knocking himself cold but taking out three of his teeth and emotionally scarring each and every kid that had been there to witness all the blood. Jessa herself had raced home, screaming hysterically to her mother that Brad had killed himself by breaking his head open.

There was the turn off the bus took to school that Jessa had sometimes grown to hate in the morning, but *always* looked forward to at the end of the day coming home.

A grassy park that had a swing set and small playground...and now what looked suspiciously like a human body. Jessa only looked long enough to make sure it wasn't moving and then made a conscious effort to ignore it completely and not give-in to her impulse to run over and check to see if it was someone she knew. Maybe even someone she had come so far to see and –

"So yeah!" Jessa said suddenly, disturbing Cade as he had begun to doze again in her arms. "We were incredibly lucky it was on a straight road and that it lasted for as long as it did. It would have been better if it had gotten us to the street and I could have just pulled into my driveway and...but it got us this far – and saved us who knows how many days of walking and...yeah."

Cade only blinked at her, seemingly quite solemn. Jessa knew she was pushing herself too hard. She hadn't slept in two days, focussed only on moving forward, feeling so close to home. But she was weak and her hands had developed this strange shake to them that worried her a little but not enough to rest.

She didn't know what was going to happen tomorrow – she had stopped imagining a future beyond getting to her mother and how she would *somehow* make everything alright.

"See that?...down there is the track I used to ride down to get to the neighbours' houses to play with the other kids. It used to take me forever to get there because we're the only house for miles around and so after a while I just stopped bothering. So then Mum started to worry I was becoming anti-social so she would offer to drive me all the way there and back...I never used to think anything about it but seriously it must have been *such* a pain in the ass...she's such a good Mum..."

"That's Aunty Marg's and Uncle Joe's place – it means we're not far now! They're weren't really my Aunt and Uncle but Mum had me call them that from when I was a little-little kid so I kind of got used to it. They were really old – even back then – and then Aunty Marg died and Uncle Joe couldn't cope with a big house so his children put him in a home and we didn't hear anything so he might still be there...or...he would have been...anyway Aunty Marg used to make her own lemonade – this incredibly sour brew that I think she used to forget to put the sugar in. And then she would make these unbelievably sweet peanut-cookie and she would pick...cashews I think they're called – only she'd get confused and pick up the salted ones and so they would have this really weird taste. But I *loved* them and still miss them – and her of course and..."

And then Jessa spotted home.

3

She came to a shuddering stop, staring at the building so hard as though waiting for it to disappear. When she got her feet moving again, it was as though her shoes had weights. Nevertheless, she started running, pitched forward at such an angle it seemed like she was fighting a gale force wind that was attempting to push her back.

Her chest began to hurt from the exertion and Cade squirmed and wriggled in her arms because she was squeezing him so tight.

"Mum! MUM!" She started screaming as soon as she made it through the gate and up the path – or at least that was how it seemed in her head. In reality she was so puffed and anxious that all that came out was a hushed gasp. "Mum – it's me! I'm home! I'm here!"

The front door was wide open as she ran inside. The back door was also lazily wining open in the slight breeze – she could see it from the front door and into the backyard. Her mother had used to joke that theirs was the kind of house that didn't encourage visitors because they could come in one door and out the other.

The dining room was on one side and walking through that, the kitchen. The living room was opposite side, then leading to a small odd shaped room that Jessa and her mother used as a bit of study/dumping ground for all the odds and ends they didn't want to pack away but didn't use on a regular basis.

Her mother's sewing machine (now lying on its side); Jessa's old high school textbooks, swept onto an overturned chair; a box of wrapping paper, her mother's sewing kit and a few steps from that, her expensive extra-sharp sewing scissors with the fancy ornate handle, now covered in dried blood.

Cade wriggled in her arms and Jessa realized she had been squeezing him again. She dumped the kid near the couch and a basket of mostly broken or badly worn toys from Jessa's childhood that her mother kept for when visitors with kids dropped by. Then Jessa kept moving, unaware of Cade watching her solemnly.

In the kitchen there were a few more signs that something bad had happened: a chair knocked askew, the knife caddy on the floor and missing two of its six knives, dishes still in the sink. The last one wasn't exactly earth-shattering thing since her mother hadn't been *that* pedantic about keeping everything spic and span, however the plates had insets crawling on them, indicating they had been there for a while. She glanced into the backyard out of habit and spied a dried dark puddle of something on the back porch but spun away so fast she was left dizzy. Upstairs it was no different – nothing out of place, but no sign of her mother either. She had then sat herself on the top step, her head in her hands.

'I don't want to be here,' Jessa decided. 'I don't want to know. I want to go now.' She had thought she had prepared for this. She had warned herself that it was a long shot that her mother would be here considering everything else had gone to hell and that just because she wanted something so desperately, didn't mean it was going to be that way.

"We'll leave," Jessa said quietly. She went into the lounge room to pick up Cade and then stopped again. "We'll leave and go...where?"

Cade had got his hands on a little toy car and was gently rolling it across the carpet. Jessa watched him for a few seconds and then tapped him on the shoulder so he would look at her and put her hands under his arms to lift him up. She sat down on the couch with him in her lap facing her and the two of them stared at each other.

"So what are we going to do *now* kid?...I think...I think I might have really screwed up here."

He reached up with one chubby fist, touching her chin like he was giving her face a high-five. This impression caused Jessa to smile despite everything. He put his head on her chest, his arms around her neck and Jessa held him. "At least we've got each other, right? No matter what, we've at least got each other."

Her chest heaved as she cried but Cade just continued to snuggled into her until they heard the noise from upstairs.

EPILOGUE –

It had turned out to be nothing but the wind causing a tree branch to drag across the side of the house. It had scared the hell out of me though, if only because I hadn't known what to wish for: Mum, alive and well after all; or Mum, nowhere near alive and like Hailey's Mum – but at least I would have known, one way or another.

But just the wind. It had taken me longer to work up with the courage to go out into the backyard and investigate the porch. It had been blood and I'd followed the trail to Danielle, a check-out chick from the local supermarket. She had been dead for a while and there hadn't been a whole lot left of her to identify after the weather and animals had gotten to her but her name tag was still on. I haven't seen any animals but I prefer this explanation to the other my mind came up with – *someone* gnawing on her. I had stared at her for a good long while.

I couldn't just leave her there – not because it wasn't the 'right' thing to do but because it felt...unsightly. Maybe my morals haven't slipped so far yet considering I couldn't stand the thought of having a dead body in the backyard, fermenting. So now she's buried in the side garden where the ground was softest. Probably one of the last 'burials' to be taking place these days. Danielle should consider herself grateful.

It's not easy but just being home again has helped far more than I thought it would.

Probably just my imagination but sometimes I feel like I can almost hear my mother's voice, telling me what to do. We can't stay forever though. It's not food or shelter that's the problem – I've already raided several of the neighbours' places and the small shop in town.

No, the problem is having to be constantly on alert and on-guard. A person can't live like this permanently. And Cade needs other people in his life of course.

And I wouldn't mind having someone else to talk to.

So while I had thought I would get home and then let the rest of the world take care of itself, that won't work. I thought it would be a relief to finally stand still and spend more than a single night in the same place but I feel antsy. Maybe I grew used to being on the move so it feels unnatural to sit still for more than a few hours. Even Cade seems out of sorts. I keep telling myself to enjoy it while I can and that I'm going to miss the luxury soon.

Because I *am* going back out on the road.

I've decided to search for Sam and his family. It's going to be one hell of a trek to get all the way back and there's no guarantee they will be where they said they were going but it's a target to aim for.

I'll leave a note for Hailey just in case by some miracle she does show up here – maybe even with her father, if miracles are being handed out!

Maybe it's actually not the right thing for Cade after all but I have to get out of here. Just the other day I thought I spotted a dead mob of about ten or so.

And I think Mum was with them.

Finished writing 15th March 2017

Finished editing 12th March 2018/21st January 2019/9th January 2020